# Storming the Castle Bridge

# Storming the Castle Bridge

The Perils of Star, the Prince, and a Dragon

By

Charles Patton

Many years ago in a land with forests and
swamps ruled by reptiles and wild beasts, near a
large old castle stood a small bridge at the center
of a looming war.

# Table of Contents

# 1. The Promise and a Creature

In the rolling hills of northwestern Pennsylvania, the summer of 1949 held secrets among the dense woods and a winding, mysterious river. Deep within the forest, a rented cabin awaited the Johnson family, promising a weekend of peace—or so they thought. As they drove toward their getaway under a cloudless blue sky, none of them suspected that one of their quiet plans would lead to a hair-raising encounter with some very peculiar creatures.

The Johnson family's maroon Hudson sedan, shaped like a slow-moving turtle, rattled off the end of an old wooden bridge and chugged along a narrow country highway, its tires humming against the road.

Star, eleven years old, had short blond hair and striking blue eyes, just like her mother's. Her father had given her the nickname Star, inspired by her tall, slender frame, which reminded him of a brittle starfish—with its long, delicate arms and a tiny center.

Star sat across the back seat from her brother, Tyrus—Ty. A year older but a few inches shorter, Ty shared their mother's slim build, blue eyes, and blond hair, though he had a distinct cowlick that refused to stay flat.

As the countryside blurred past, Star fidgeted with a small lead troll figurine, its worn edges cool in her hands. Around Ty's neck hung a cream-colored skull on a string, faintly glowing in the shadows of the car.

The two siblings were deep into a road game.

"W!" Ty shouted suddenly.

"Where?" Star asked her slightly raspy voice laced with a soft southern drawl.

"White cow," he said, pointing to a dairy cow grazing lazily in a nearby field.

"Colors don't count, only letters on signs, you twerp. You're cheatin'," Star snapped.

Ty ignored her, pulling two bottles of soda pop from the portable ice chest on the floor between them. Using the metal handle at the chest's edge, he pried off both caps with a practiced motion and pushed one bottle toward her.

"Get that away from me!" she said, leaning as far back as the car seat allowed.

"What's your problem?" Ty asked, frowning.

Up front, their mother, Betty, poured coffee from a Thermos™ and handed it to their father, Bill, who took it with a nod.

Betty turned to the back seat, her tone calm but firm. "Ty, stop teasing your sister."

Star crossed her arms and frowned. "Who knows what's in that?" she said, pointing at the soda. "And look at the color—natural orange juice isn't even that bright. It's unnatural, and I'm not drinking it anymore. You have my word on that."

"That's a laugh," Ty said, smirking.

Betty tried to reassure her. "Honey, it's mostly soda water and sugar."

Bill glanced in the rearview mirror. "Star, it's open. Don't waste it."

Star crossed her arms, her voice firm. "I said I wouldn't drink that unnatural stuff again. When I give my word, it's final."

"Calm down," Bill yelled, his patience thinning. "Just drink it. It's already open."

With a sharp glare, Star snatched the bottle from Ty, took the tiniest sip, and shoved it back at him. "On my word, I'll get even," she hissed.

"You never keep your word," Ty whispered with a grin.

Star turned to her father, her tone serious. "I need to get better at keeping my word. How can I do that?"

"Here's our road," Bill announced.

The Hudson turned onto a dusty, one-lane dirt
road cutting through the woods, a thick cloud
of dust billowing in its wake.

The car jolted along the uneven trail when a
blur of toffee-colored fur suddenly darted across
their path.

Bill slammed on the brakes, jerking the car to a
halt. The kids leaned forward, craning over the
back of the front seat, then turned to peer out
the rear window.

Betty squinted toward the roadside. "Was that a
raccoon?"

Bill frowned, checking the rearview mirror as
his eyes searched for another glimpse. "Wrong
color for a raccoon," he said. "The locals tell
stories about strange creatures in these hills."

"Now, don't go scaring the children," Betty said.

"They won't be able to sleep tonight."

## 2.  Sparkles and Spats

Dust swirled as the Hudson rolled onto the dry grass between the road and a fence, coming to a stop. Everyone piled out of the car. Bill grabbed an unlit kerosene lantern and a suitcase, then walked toward the fence. He pushed one of the weathered wooden posts down and stepped on it, flattening the barbed wire against the ground.

Betty retrieved a picnic basket and some blankets from the trunk, then followed him carefully over the fence. She paused, looking back to make sure the kids were following.

"Cabin's this way," Bill called over his shoulder as he tramped off into the woods. Within moments, the trees swallowed him from sight.

Meanwhile, Ty pulled a package of firecrackers from his pocket, along with a wooden match. Striking the match on the sole of his shoe, he lit the fuse and tossed the firecrackers onto the dirt road behind Star. The quiet shattered as they exploded. Star jumped and spun around, her heart racing.

"Ty!" Betty yelled, admonishing him.

"Why do you torment me?" Star asked.

"'Cause it's so easy," Ty replied with a smirk.

Star scrunched her face, silently wishing she'd find the courage to stand up to her brother one day. Nearby, one of the firecrackers that hadn't exploded continued spinning, fizzing, and spraying sparkles.

"Why didn't that one explode?" she asked Ty.

"I guess because it was packed loosely or the fuse was loose," he said.

"Like your brain?" she shot back.

Ty ignored her, grabbing a small suitcase as he and Betty started down the path. Just before disappearing into the woods, Betty glanced back at Star.

Star stood watching them leave but didn't follow.

"Don't go wandering off," Betty called over her shoulder as the trees seemed to swallow her up. "You could get lost in these parts—and don't go down by the river alone."

# 3.   Bridge to Trouble

"Okay, okay," Star shouted back, her voice echoing through the trees. She veered downhill, away from the direction her family had taken.

Butterflies fluttered in lazy patterns as she strolled along the dirt road, and a bright red cardinal zigzagged across her path.
The quiet and the scenery wrapped around her, giving her a rare, carefree moment. She rounded a bend and came upon a striking wrought iron bridge in the shape of a giant Y over a narrow slow-flowing river. Fancy

carved stone columns supported it, and intricate metal railings lined its edges.

The three narrow roads converged at the bridge's center, each forming one branch of the Y. At the junction stood a fountain, its stillness hinting at the absence of traffic. Star frowned, wondering why the roads seemed far too narrow for cars.

Curious, she climbed over the guardrail and made her way down the embankment, enjoying the sweeping view of the river. She picked up a few pebbles and tossed them into the water below, the soft splashes punctuating the stillness. Eventually, she sat down, leaning against the sturdy trunk of an oak tree atop the embankment. She watched the water, calm and steady, flowing south where two rivers from the north merged beneath the bridge.

She lost herself in the moment until a rustling in the grass behind her jolted her back to reality. Star spun around so quickly that it seemed she floated for a moment.

Losing her balance, she tumbled down the embankment toward the river.

Panic gripped her as she slid, the thought of falling into the water terrifying—she didn't know how to swim.

As she rolled toward the river, two unusual critters grabbed hold of her, stopping her fall. One stood about six inches shorter than Star, who was four feet five inches tall, and the other about a foot shorter. The critters walked on two legs and looked like large teddy bears. They had round eyes, round ears, and soft fur with subtle patterns.

The taller one, pale green, wore a flower-print shirt, while the shorter one, light brown, sported a tan vest. Barely visible markings appeared in their fur: the green critter had darker green stripes, and the brown one had kidney-bean-shaped spots, each about the size of a quarter.

Nearby, a small cart, the size a goat might pull, stood covered by a tarp.

Frightened, Star stared at the critters.

"You okay?" the pale green one asked in a high-pitched voice.

Star jumped, startled.

"I'm Toffee," the brown critter said, trying to break the tension. "And he's Cucumber."

Star hesitated, then sniffed the air and tentatively smelled their forearms, first one, then the other. "You smell like your names," she said, puzzled.

Cucumber and Toffee sniffed each other and shrugged, seemingly unsure of what she meant. A few lime-colored bugs with dark green stripes buzzed around Cucumber, and he swatted at them absentmindedly.

Star, uncertain about the strange creatures, glanced around to see if there were others and took a small step back. "I'm Star," she said cautiously. "Where did you come from?"

"Wurzenburg, that village there," Toffee said in a low voice, pointing to the upstream land where two rivers met at the Y's center.

Star's eyes widened as she spotted a village and a castle for the first time. She blinked, confused. How had she not seen them before? Were they always there? Was she dreaming? She pinched herself.

She wasn't.

Now more worried than ever, she studied the scene. The village was made of stone buildings with cobblestone streets. Behind it loomed a dark, ominous castle. Its broken spires and a rickety central tower gave it a stormy, foreboding appearance, especially with the skull image near the top. The bridge cast a shadow over much of the village.

"I didn't see that little burg before . . . or the castle," Star said nervously.

"Ah, yes. The old Black Castle," Cucumber said. "The only castle in these parts."

"So, what are you? Trolls?" Star asked, raising an eyebrow.

"No! No! We're not trolls!" Cucumber exclaimed, offended.

"Just because we live near a bridge doesn't make us trolls!" Toffee added. "We hate being called trolls!"

"We're sprites," Cucumber clarified. "Not elves, not gremlins, and definitely not trolls."

"Sorry. I didn't know being a troll was a bad thing," Star said.

From behind the cart, two small critters that looked like hedgehogs peeked out. One was pink, the other blue, each about the size of a bowling ball. They scurried up to stand behind Cucumber, their four feet hidden as they moved. Their faces barely protruded from their round bodies.

"Don't tell me they're trolls," Star said, eyeing them skeptically.

"No, not trolls! Imps!" Cucumber corrected.

"Not trolls! Not trolls!" the imps echoed in unison.

"Trolls have giants for relatives," Cucumber added.

"And scare little kids who walk across bridges,"
Toffee said. "We like kids."

"Sprites just go about their business,"
Cucumber said.

"With their imps in tow. What business is
that?" Star asked, steering the conversation
away from the sensitive topic.

"Ah, well . . . ah, trading . . ." Toffee began.

"I guess you could call us merchants,"
Cucumber said.

Both sprites glanced around nervously. Star
noticed their unease and began looking around,
too.

# 4. Sprites, Imps, and Secrets

"And what business are you in?" Cucumber asked. Star thought for a moment.

"I'm looking for a, uh, symbol," she said.

"Oh, you're a musician," Toffee said.

"No, not a cymbal." Star clapped her hands to indicate the motion of hitting two cymbals together. "I meant a, ah, a sign."

"Oh then you're a painter," Toffee said.

"Never mind," Star said. Cucumber and Toffee glanced at each other with a mysterious guilt and occasionally looked over their shoulders at the river.

"If you have to leave, I think I'm okay now," Star said. "Thanks for keeping me out of the river. I can't swim and I'm afraid of the water."

"Think nothing of it. We're just waiting for Old Sage to pick us up," Cucumber said.

"Who is Old Sage?" Star asked.

"The ferry tender," Toffee said, his back to the river as he pointed over his shoulder with his thumb.

"He's a fairy?" Star asked, teasing, not having seen the boat coming yet.

"No. No. A sprite. He operates the ferryboat that takes us to the village," Cucumber said. He winked to signal he was catching on to her sense of humor.

Star smiled when she realized Cucumber understood her teasing. Her smile then faded and she looked up toward where the sun was in the sky – to get an idea of the time of day. She would need to return to the family's cabin soon – but how could she leave until she learned more about the village and these critters.

"You called the ferry tender Old Sage. Is that his name?" Star asked.

"Everyone calls him Old Sage," Toffee said.

"Because, well, he's old."

"No one calls him that to his face," Cucumber said, "But I think he knows what others call him."

Old Sage steered and powered his ferryboat in their direction. Star looked over the very ornamental and mechanically elaborate ferryboat. Inwardly, she worried about what she was doing – about whether she might get trapped in this world of critters and not be able to return to her family.

"It's kind of a small boat, designed to handle goat carts and wheelbarrows and similar small-wheeled equipment," Toffee said.

To power the boat's paddlewheel contraption, Old Sage pedaled with his feet and pumped a bar up and down with his hands when steering did not interfere. While steering, he pushed a long rudder with his strong right arm from one side to the other when he needed to change the ferry's direction. Star could see that the ferryboat was an engineering marvel with lots of gadgets.

"Here he is now," Toffee said.

Old Sage guided the ferryboat to the shore. His fur was darker green than Cucumber's fur and showed gray around his muzzle, not unlike a beard. His fur revealed a pattern of nuts and bolts.

"Hail hearty!" Old Sage hollered, greeting his two regular passengers.

"Hail, Captain!" Cucumber called.

With the ferryboat pulled up to the shore, Old Sage worked a crude mechanical device that caused a gangplank to extend out from the boat. Old Sage stayed seated in his captain's chair, which, being higher than anything else on the boat, afforded him a good view all around.

"Coming?" Toffee asked as he turned to Star and invited her along. He, Cucumber and the Imps all boarded the ferry via the gangplank.

She glanced up the hill in the direction from which she had come with a worried look, again checked the position of the sun in the sky then looked to the others.

"How often does the ferryboat run?" she asked.

"Every two hours by day, every four at night," Old Sage said.

"He's very punctual, used to be an engineer," Toffee said.

"I heard that! I'm still an engineer, you whippersnapper!" Old Sage yelled over the sound of the engine.

"Seems like a lot of trips, and only you two here and about?" Star asked.

"It's public transportation. It doesn't need to make sense," Old Sage said.

"He mostly carries workers between the opposite shore over there and the village," Toffee said and gestured to small shacks on the east side of the river.

"I hadn't noticed those before," Star said.

"All aboard, if you're comin' aboard," Old Sage hollered. "We're ready to go."

"Maybe you can find a symbol over there," Cucumber said.

"Do I dare to go on this boat?" Star asked herself aloud.

She glanced over her shoulder, toward where she had ventured away from her family.

"Just for a short while. I've got to return here in two hours, on the next ferry. Okay?" She walked toward the gangway. She could not help but worry about what she was getting herself into.

# 5. Crossing Paths with Courage

Cucumber, Toffee, and the two imps climbed aboard the ferry. Star hesitated at the gangplank, uneasy about walking over the water. She glanced back once more, then scooted up the plank without looking down.

Once aboard, Star joined Cucumber and Toffee at the front of the boat, away from where Old Sage might overhear them.

"They convicted his father for being a coward during the last war," Toffee said. "Of course, Old Sage was too young to attend the trial, and his father didn't show up for it anyway."

Star frowned, confused. "Last war?" she asked.

"Most think cowardice runs in his family," Cucumber added.

Star's instincts flared. She didn't believe them. "He doesn't seem cowardly to me," she said firmly.

"His family tried over and over to overturn the conviction," Toffee said. "But the queen wouldn't allow a retrial."

"He's haunted by how they treated his father," Cucumber said.

Star left them and wandered to the rear of the ferryboat as it passed under the bridge's girders. She paused, admiring the craftsmanship of the bridge's structure.

"Yeow!" Star yelped, stumbling over a coiled rope.

"Watch your step!" Old Sage hollered.

Before she could respond, four large gray-and-white seagull-like birds swooped down from the girders. Their long, thin beaks and folded legs gave them an unusual, elegant appearance. Star gasped, convinced they were heading straight for her, and dove onto the deck.

Old Sage chuckled and looked up. "They won't hurt you, deary. Them's albagulls—friends of mine. It's a family: mom, dad, and two kids."

"They all look like adults to me," Star said, peeking up from the deck.

The albagulls soared high, then swooped down again, this time skimming just above Old Sage's head. He didn't flinch. Instead, he raised his arm, letting his hand glide across their bodies as they passed.

Star climbed to her feet and sat next to Old Sage's chair, watching as he gazed fondly at the birds.

"I gave them their family name, the Trumpets, 'cause that's the sound they make when they get excited," Old Sage said with a grin.

He mimicked pulling the rope on a truck horn with his fist, and the Trumpets responded with a blast that sounded like a cavalry trumpet call.

Star tilted her head, studying him. "You seem different."

"You mean from those sprites? I am," Old Sage said, laughing. "I'm from a village far downstream."

Star scanned the horizon ahead, her gaze distant.

"Looking for something?" Old Sage asked.

"A symbol of courage," Star said quietly, her voice tinged with longing.

"You're not alone," Old Sage replied with a knowing nod.

# 6.  Whispers and Warnings

Traveling mid-river on the ferry, Star sat with Cucumber and Toffee at the bow, gazing toward the village ahead. When she glanced back, she noticed Old Sage slipping what looked like a note into a bottle and sealing it with a small wooden plug.

She nudged Cucumber and silently gestured toward Old Sage. Toffee caught the signal too, and the three of them watched intently as Old Sage slid the bottle over the side into the water. He glanced around to see if anyone was watching, but they quickly turned away, avoiding his gaze.

As the ferry approached the village, Star noticed a dock extending perpendicularly from a street running along the riverbank. From her vantage point, she saw the village filling the point of land where the two rivers merged. Its main street paralleled the rivers, and on the opposite side of the street stood an assortment of charming shops and offices.

The village captured her attention with its quaint atmosphere. The buildings were scaled to fit the residents, most of whom appeared to be less than three feet tall. She read the lettering on nearby shop windows: *Port Authority: Pay All Tariffs Here*, *Fresh Fish*, and *Boats Not for Hire*.

As the ferry neared the dock, and they transferred into a small boat, Cucumber and Toffee whispered nervously, fidgeting as they noticed several port officials waiting. The officials wore vests adorned with three yellow sergeant stripes on their sleeves, and similar but fainter patterns were visible on their blue fur.

Star turned her attention to the village ahead. Three streets extended from the dock: one riverside street wound left, climbing a hill before disappearing around a corner; a second street cut through the row of shops and headed directly toward the Black Castle, which loomed under the shadow of the bridge. The third street ran to the right, curving around the village.

An old sign with an arrow pointing up the middle street read *To Castle*, while a newer sign pointing to the right read *To King's Palace*.


As the boat pulled to the dock, Cucumber and Toffee grew so agitated that they seemed ready to leap overboard. Suddenly, a commotion erupted from the street leading from the dock. The port officials, distracted, hurried toward the noise.

The moment the boat touched the dock, Cucumber and Toffee bolted off with their cart.

"Where are you going?" Star hollered after them.

"No time to explain. Maybe we'll see you later," Cucumber called back.

"But I need your help!" she shouted, her voice laced with frustration.

Already out of earshot, they disappeared up the hill, one pulling the cart and the other pushing while the imps scurried after them.

Annoyed at being left behind, Star planted her hands on her hips, glaring after them.

"Any suggestions where I should go from here?" she asked Old Sage.

"I wish I did. Just stay away from the old Castle," he warned. "It's in bad shape and might collapse any day now."

"I'll see you on your next trip," Star said.

"You sure?" he called back, his voice tinged with something unsaid.

"You've got my word," she replied, then added softly, "I hope."

As Star stepped off the gangplank, the imps almost knocked her over in haste to catch up with Cucumber and Toffee. By the time she reached the street, she could barely see them vanishing up the hill and around the bend.

Drawn by the commotion, Star followed the noise to a gathering of townsfolk surrounding a public speaker. She noticed that the villagers' fur bore patterns—fish, vegetables, bread— symbolizing their trades.

Star edged closer to listen but ended up perilously near the water's edge, one misstep from falling in.

"The Westsiders are preparing for war again, and the Eastsiders know they are!" the speaker declared loudly from atop a soapbox.

"How do you know?" asked the taller of two officials.

"I saw them with my own eyes! They're making arrows by the hundreds," the speaker replied.

"This is terrible news. Someone should tell the king," the shorter official said.

"Not me. I'd tell the king if it weren't for the queen," the speaker muttered, stepping back.

"Hush! You shouldn't talk like that in public," the taller official warned.

"Right, you are. I like my head where it is," the speaker said, stepping down from the box.

The port officials conferred, gesturing about who should report to the king, but neither volunteered.

A bystander bumped into Star, nearly knocking her into the water. She teetered on the edge before stumbling forward. Pressing her hand to her pounding heart, she turned to see where she'd almost fallen.

A blond-furred critter stood on a nearby boat. The critter's muscular build and long, rounded-pointy ears, sticking through the brim of a white straw hat, set him apart from the villagers. The hat reminded Star of her mother's, filling her with a pang of longing.

"Careful," the blond critter said.

"Thanks," Star replied, glancing back at the water's edge.

"No, I meant who you hang out with," he added.

"You mean Cucumber and Toffee?" she asked, confused.

"They're notorious," the blond critter said, baiting her curiosity.

"Oh my! Tell me about them," Star said, her voice laced with worry, fearing what she might learn.

## 7.   Lines in the Sand

"Better come aboard. The story's not for public ears," the blond critter said.

Star hesitated but walked cautiously onto the gangplank and boarded the boat. Painted on the bow was its name: ***River Trader***. Stowed on deck were open crates holding live groundhogs, prairie dogs, and tiny kangaroos called wallabies. Alongside these were kegs of nails, bales of hay, bolts of cloth, and pails containing yet more bolts.

"I'm Zuke. Have a seat," the blond critter said, motioning to a keg.

"I'm Star," she replied, shaking his hand and sitting down. "Sounds like those Eastsiders and Westsiders are stirring up trouble. Who are they?"

"The Eastsiders live about five lomits up the right fork, on the opposite bank," Zuke explained, pointing upriver. "The Westsiders are the same distance up the left fork."

"What's their beef?" Star asked.

"Cows have nothing to do with it," Zuke replied, confused.

"No, I mean, what are they upset about?" Star clarified.

"The bridge," Zuke said.

Meanwhile, the queen sat with Eastsider elders under a canopy tent. Her dark gray fur bore white skull patterns, and her tall, thin frame towered over the others. A topknot of fur curled into a cowlick atop her head. The elders, whose lighter gray fur was marked with dark skulls, avoided her gaze as she paced.

"How shall we go about it?" one elder asked hesitantly.

"Better than last time, I hope!" the queen snapped.

"We need a new strategy," the elder said, his voice timid.

"You've tried and failed to control that bridge repeatedly!" the queen yelled, glaring.

An aide entered the tent and bowed. "Your Majesty, I've heard that a downstream village may have created a new weapon."

"What is it?" the queen demanded.

"I don't know," the aide admitted, shrugging.

Disgusted, she scowled. The aide backed away, visibly shrinking under her glare.

"Find that weapon before the Eastsiders do. No one will stand in my way this time. Do you understand?" she shouted at the elder.

"Yes, Your Highness," he said, bowing before retreating.

The queen stormed off, muttering to herself. "Let the king keep his village around the castle. I will rule all the surrounding lands." Her dark cape billowed dramatically behind her as she disappeared.


Aboard the *River Trader*, Zuke and Star remained on the kegs.

"The Eastsiders and Westsiders are vying for control of the bridge," Zuke explained.

"Why?" Star asked.

"To tax vendors as they cross with goods."

"Are you Eastsider or Westsider?" Star asked, suddenly suspicious.

"Neither. I'm from a village so far upstream, it doesn't even have a name," Zuke said.

Star laughed nervously. "So now we hear about a third direction—some weirdness from the north."

"Fourth, if you count the DoubleYews downstream," Zuke added.

Star noticed Old Sage sneaking away from the dock with a sack slung over his shoulder. "Is he from your area?" she asked.

"No, he's downstream—from the village of cowards," Zuke replied, irritated.

Star frowned. "No wonder I liked him," she muttered to herself. She turned to Zuke, "They say he's from the most renowned family of cowards. Is that how you see him?"

"His father fled during the last war," Zuke admitted reluctantly.

Star pressed for details, but Zuke shrugged, avoiding the subject.

Their conversation shifted to Cucumber and Toffee. Zuke revealed, "They're smugglers—

sneaking in goods people can't afford because of high taxes or quotas."

"Smuggling? That's not honorable," Star said, pacing.

Zuke shrugged. "Tariffs, taxes, and fees are just lines in the sand."

"What do they smuggle?" Star asked.

"Root beer, orange soda, and caffeine drinks," Zuke said.

Angered, Star said, "And I thought they could help me find courage!"

Cucumber and Toffee returned to the dock area, flanked by officials. As Star and Zuke watched, the officials boarded *River Trader*.

"You're accomplices," one official said, grabbing Zuke and Star.

"Wait! I have nothing to do with this!" Star protested.

The officials pushed them off the boat, marched them down the street, and ignored Star's frantic questions. The Imps followed, chirping, "To the king! To the king!"

Star glanced around nervously. "Are they taking us to the Black Castle?" she whispered.

"No," Zuke said calmly. "That's just a market now."



Back at the family cabin, time passed slowly. Betty put away groceries while Bill tinkered with a fishing line. Ty grabbed a soda and wandered outside. Betty glanced out the window, wondering where Star had gone.

# 8.   Plots and Prisoners

In her chamber, the queen leaned over three sinister-looking critters, speaking in a voice too low for anyone else to hear. Being taller, she bent forward, staring directly into their faces. The three wore dark vests over their gray fur and black hats pulled low over their heads. The skull patterns on their fur were similar to, but slightly different from, those on the queen's fur.

Outside the chamber, the king's counsel pressed his ear to the door. His deep, dark, scarlet fur bore a barely noticeable pattern of scales, like those used to measure justice.

Inside, the queen turned and left the three standing in the shadows. She walked to a spinning wheel, sat down, and began spinning black wool into yarn. The motion was purely mechanical, something to keep her hands busy while she thought.

The queen's daughter, the princess Cinnamon, perched nearby on a stool and moved closer to help. Cinnamon's pink fur, patterned with light red hearts, bore no resemblance to her mother's. She brushed her fur with a golden-handled brush as she spoke.

"Cinnamon, you will say nothing about this meeting, do you hear? Or you will face my wrath," the queen said without looking at her.

"I've just lost another suitor; all you care about is your Eastsider buddies! Can't you help me find another prince to court me?" Cinnamon said, exasperated.

"It wouldn't do any good. You spent all of the last one's money," the queen replied, clearly tired of her daughter's antics.

Cinnamon pouted, brushing her fur with exaggerated strokes. "But that was only my fifth one!"

"I doubt there are any eligible bachelors left in this kingdom," the queen said dryly.

"Woe is me!" Cinnamon cried dramatically.

"You might consider becoming a nun," the queen suggested with thinly veiled annoyance.

Cinnamon huffed, then walked toward the door. At the threshold, she turned back, tossing her hair. "We'll keep looking," she said before leaving.

Outside, the king's counsel slipped into the shadows as Cinnamon passed. Then, he resumed listening at the door.

Inside, the queen returned to the three Eastsiders in the shadows. "Now that she's gone, what more can you tell me?"

One of them whispered in her ear.

"If that rumor is true, we must take control of the Black Castle. Forget the bridge!" the queen exclaimed, stepping back.

The Eastsiders exchanged glances and nodded.

"Get your agents downriver and investigate that rumor. Bring back all the material you can find and report to me immediately," the queen ordered.

Outside, the king's counsel slipped away just as the Eastsiders prepared to leave.


About that time, Star and her fellow prisoners arrived at the king's palace. To her surprise, it resembled an ornate office building rather than a grand royal estate. The massive front doors, taller than Star, were guarded by elite guards with deep blue fur patterned with stars. They wore gold belts, cross-straps, and scabbards with short swords.

The officials marched their prisoners to the guards. "We have criminals to present to the king for swift justice," one announced.

The guards ceremoniously drew their swords, presenting arms before allowing the group to pass.

Inside, the prisoners were led down a long corridor to another set of ornate doors flanked by more guards.

"We're here to see the king," the official said.

One guard knocked twice. The door cracked open, revealing the blue-furred face of another guard.

"Port officials with prisoners to see the king," he announced.

"Prisoners?" Star muttered, glaring at Zuke as she swatted his arm.

"Take it easy, kid," Zuke said, pulling his arm back.

"I've got to get back to the ferry! What will the king do to us?" Star asked anxiously.

At the family cabin, time passed slowly in its separate dimension. Betty frequently glanced at her watch and out the window, clearly worried.

The palace's ornate doors swung open, revealing a massive room with marble pillars and a high, decorated ceiling. Multicolored courtiers formed a corridor leading to the throne, where a rotund king sat. His royal purple fur displayed a pattern of pale yellow flowers. A gold crown rest on his head between his round furr ears. To his right sat the bored prince, his lighter purple fur echoing the king's colors. To his far left, beyond the queen's empty chair, sat the princess. The king's counsel stood behind the throne.

"Can we escape?" Star whispered to Zuke.

"Silence in the presence of the king!" the king's counsel barked.

The counsel descended from the throne, stopping before the prisoners. "What are the charges?" he asked.

"Smuggling to avoid tariffs," the arresting official said.

"Where's the evidence?"

"Their cart rolled down the hill, spilling its contents. People grabbed what they could and fled," the official admitted sheepishly.

"So, you have none. What do you say for yourselves?" the king asked, addressing the captives.

"We were framed! The cart wasn't ours—it was his," Cucumber said, pointing at Zuke.

"Is that true?" the king asked.

"Check your harbor records," Zuke replied calmly. "Your port officials inspected my boat this morning and found it in full tariff compliance."

"We already did that," the king's counsel said, stepping forward. He poked Zuke's chest with a finger. "The report shows that you imported hogs, dogs, and bees but paid no tariffs."

"How could that be when we charge ten percent for hogs and dogs and five percent on bees?" the king asked, his voice rising in anger.

"They're groundhogs, not pig hogs," Zuke said evenly. "They're wallabies, not honeybees. And they're prairie dogs, not pet dogs."

"None of which require fees," the king nodded.

The king shot his counsel a displeased look. The flustered counsel turned to an assistant. "Make a note to close those loopholes," he said, then faced Toffee. "What's your story?"

"I'm with him," Toffee said, pointing toward Cucumber.

The king's attention shifted to Star. "And you're new to my kingdom. What did you do?" the king's counsel asked.

"Nothing. I just rode over on the ferry and was talking with Zuke here…" Star said nervously, fearing what punishment might await.

"Who else rode the ferry with you?" the king's counsel pressed.

"Uhh… Old Sage," Star said cautiously.

"Was anyone else on the ferry with you?" the king's counsel asked again.

"Yes… those two Imps," Star admitted.

"Smooth move," Zuke whispered to Star.

The king's counsel clasped his hands behind his back, pacing as he spoke aloud. "You said Zuke framed you two, but we inspected Zuke's boat and found it clean. We have no evidence. And you," he gestured to Star, "just came for a visit. So… the Imps did it?"

"Imps did it! Imps did it!" the Imps squealed, spinning in mock protest.

Exasperated, the king's counsel turned to the king. "Your Majesty, what should be done with these miscreants?"

The king stroked his chin thoughtfully, staring upward as he pondered. Before he could speak, the first official, agitated, stepped forward.

"Your Majesty, I have urgent news to deliver while you consider their fate."

"Speak," the king commanded.

"One of our townsfolk saw the Eastsiders making new weapons for war—and the Westsiders are doing the same," the official reported.

"It's the bridge again!" the second official exclaimed.

The king rose and began pacing. "This is dreadful," he said. "The last time they went to war, our lives were disrupted horribly. The rivers were fouled, arrows from the bridge riddled our villagers, and we couldn't venture beyond the valley for food without risking death."

"Did you know of this pending war?" the king asked, turning to his counsel.

"You might ask the queen. She may have heard something," the counsel suggested, carefully avoiding mention of his eavesdropping.

"The queen… hmmm. We've been at odds for months over this war situation. Very well—send for the queen!" the king ordered.

"Send for the queen!" the king's counsel barked to the servants.

"Send for the queen! Send for the queen!" the Imps mimicked.

The king glared at the Imps, and they scurried behind Cucumber.

Servants hurried out of the court.

"Nothing is good about war," the king mused aloud while waiting for the queen. "You give up the comfort of family, the joy of watching your children grow, the delight of music, and the rapture of good food."

"But war is a great forum for creating heroes and displaying courage," the king's counsel offered.

"There must be a better place to show courage," Star said quietly.

"Silence in the presence of the king!" a guard shouted.

Star cringed, retreating into herself.

## 9.   Sentenced to War

"It is a greater courage to save lives than to take them," the king said. "The DoubleYews are the only ones who seem to understand that."

"Those cowards!" the king's counsel scoffed. "They run from trouble."

"Perhaps that's a story with another chapter," Prince Concord said.

Surprised, the king turned to his son as the prince rarely spoke.

"All in good time," the king said, walking over to pat the prince's shoulder.

The servants returned, and the large side doors swung open. Everyone except the king and the prisoners fell to the floor in deference as the queen swept in behind them, clutching her scepter, which was topped with a skull.

"What is this outrageous disturbance of my beauty sleep?" the queen demanded as she approached the king.

A few in the court snickered, but they fell silent and serious when the queen's sharp gaze darted their way.

"The swamp awaits," she said in a low, menacing voice.

"Swamp awaits! Swamp awaits!" the cheerful Imps chirped.

"That's right, you little twerps," the queen snapped and, with a swift kick, sent the pink Imp tumbling across the room.

The queen turned her attention to the prisoners.

"Who are these ne'er-do-wells?" she asked.

"A momentary nuisance," the king replied. "They are not why I sent for you."

"We had a report that the Eastsiders and Westsiders are arming for war again," the king's counsel said. "Do you know about this?"

The queen hesitated, thinking carefully.

"Well," she began slowly. "They've been at odds with each other for years."

Her fingers crept up her scepter, tracing the eye sockets of the skull on top.

"They both want the castle—I mean the bridge—and neither wants the other to have it," she said, carefully choosing her words. She began to pace.

"They meet at the center of the bridge and fight until both sides run out of energy and resources. Then they retreat to their villages," the queen continued, abruptly wheeling around to face the king. "So, what's new?"

"A rumor says it might be different this time—
that the old castle has some new significance.
Do you know why?" the king asked, probing.

The queen feigned ignorance, shrugging. "It's
no secret that some citizens would like this
settled once and for all," she said coyly.

"War must be avoided at all costs," the king
declared. "With our food stores at their lowest
levels in years and our population at its highest,
our losses would be catastrophic."

"What about this group here?" the king's
counsel asked impatiently, unintentionally
helping the queen by changing the subject.

The queen strode over to Star, who cowered
under her fierce gaze. Sensing Star's fear, the
queen hooked a bony finger under the girl's
chin, lifting her face to meet her own. She
leaned in menacingly.

"Throw them into the dragon swamp," the
queen commanded.

"There's a dragon here?" Star whispered tensely to Zuke.

The king pondered for a moment before addressing Zuke directly.

"We can't let crime go unpunished," the king said.

"Perhaps we could provide Your Highness with some community service," Zuke suggested.

"The only service we need is to stop the war," the king replied.

The king's counsel leaned in and whispered something in the king's ear.

"My counsel suggests feeding you to the dragon," the king said.

"Feeding us to the dragon?" Star repeated, wide-eyed, glancing nervously at Zuke.

"Feed the dragon! Feed the dragon!" the Imps chanted gleefully, dancing in circles.

"We'd be happy to take on the service of stopping the war," Zuke interjected.

"We can't stop a war between thousands of Eastsiders and Westsiders," Cucumber protested.

"We didn't do anything wrong!" Star cried.

"Irrelevant!" the king's counsel barked.

The king ignored his counsel's interruption. "All right," he said. "Your sentence is to stop the war. My son, Prince Concord, will go with you to ensure you fulfill your commitment."

The prince's eyes widened in disbelief.

"Let no harm come to him while in your care," the king's counsel warned, "or your punishment will be far worse than being dragon feed."

To emphasize his point, the counsel ran a hand under his chin in a cutting motion.

"Off with you!" the king commanded, dismissing them.

The guards seized the prisoners and escorted them out. Star, near panic, struggled to keep

calm as she was dragged from the king's
presence.

# 10. The Black Castle's Secrets

Elsewhere, a camp with rows of tents bustled with activity. Blacksmiths worked diligently over hot fires, hammering metal arrowheads into shape. In a large tent, the Westsider leader, General Sance, taller than the others and bearing light blue fur patterned with pale yellow flowers, addressed his lieutenants around a table.

"The Eastsiders are preparing for war again," General Sance said. "We have fought them over the bridge before and will fight them again."

A Westsider hurried in, saluted, and handed a dispatch to the general. General Sance read it silently, his brow furrowing. He turned to the lieutenant on his right.

"Send a squad downstream immediately. The Eastsiders are after something, and we must find out what it is," the general ordered.

At the palace, the king's guards shoved Cucumber, Toffee, and Star into the street. The prince, however, was waved out by the king's counsel and guards, avoiding any rough treatment. The Imps scurried behind.

Star stomped on Cucumber's foot.

"Yow!" Cucumber yelped.

"You dragged me into this," Star said.

"We didn't mean to!" Cucumber replied, sidestepping another stomp.

"You dragged in Zuke, too," Star added, her voice sharp.

Zuke smiled faintly, appreciating that Star was defending him.

"Well, it goes with his territory," Cucumber shrugged.

Zuke frowned.

"What a mess you got me into. You… you Trolls!" Star exclaimed.

"I'm not a Troll!" Toffee said indignantly.

"Not a Troll! Not a Troll!" the Imps chimed in.

As they walked toward the dock, Cucumber asked, "How can we make it up to you?"

"You can start by figuring out how to stop the war," Star snapped.

"You mean how *we're* going to stop it," Zuke corrected.

"Not me," Star said. "I've got a ferry to catch."

"A fairy?" Cucumber teased, holding his hand at waist height with a smirk.

"A ferryboat," Star said, annoyed.

They continued in silence for a while until Zuke spoke.

"The king said something odd," he began.

"What?" Toffee asked.

"About the war being different this time. What did the general mean?" Zuke asked.

"That something might be different this time," Cucumber said unhelpfully.

Zuke grabbed him by the scruff of his neck.

"Tell us what you know!" Zuke demanded.

"They have a magic powder," Cucumber confessed.

"A what?" Toffee asked.

"A mixture of three kinds of ground-up rocks that the DoubleYews discovered," Cucumber explained.

"Rocks? From that downstream village of whiners and worriers?" Zuke asked skeptically.

"That's why they call them DoubleYews, isn't it?" Prince Concord chimed in.

"Nobody asked you, smart-aleck!" Toffee retorted, sticking his face close to the prince's.

Cucumber grabbed Toffee and pulled him back. "Easy, boy."

"Why did the king really send you with us?" Zuke asked the prince.

"Right of passage, real-world experience, mingling with common folks—take your pick," Prince Concord replied, feigning disinterest.

"But you don't think you need such experiences?" Zuke pressed.

"Not really," the prince said nonchalantly.

"He's hopelessly spoiled," Toffee muttered, turning his back on the prince.

"Don't you think we should focus on stopping a war?" Star interjected, frustrated.

They continued walking along the river.

"They wrap a fistful of this magic powder in a tight cloth, light it, and toss it," Cucumber explained. "It explodes with a loud bang, creating a rush of gas that knocks things over. Anything close enough gets showered with sparkles and disintegrates into dust."

"From the top of the castle with that stuff," Zuke mused, "you could control the bridge."

"And the entire surrounding area," Prince Concord added.

"That's why they're fighting again—they want the Black Castle," Star said.

"So, the fight is over the castle," Cucumber concluded.

They all were lost in thought for a few minutes.

"Stopping the war is simple, then. Eliminate the castle," Zuke suggested.

"Knock it down with the magic powder?" Toffee asked skeptically.

"If it's powerful enough, if you could get enough of it, and if you knew how to use it, maybe," Star said, thinking of her brother's stories about explosives.

"That's a lot of ifs," Cucumber said.

"Lot of ifs! Lot of ifs!" the Imps echoed gleefully.

As the dock came into view, Star noticed Old Sage's shadowy figure heading back from the Black Castle, counting money. When he realized he was being watched, he hid the money and hurried off.

"Old Sage! Come back! I need to get to the other side!" Star yelled.

"You can't leave now. We made a promise," Zuke said, grabbing her arm.

"What? You made the promise to pay for a crime I didn't commit!" Star said, yanking her arm free.

"It doesn't matter how it came to be. Our word is an unbreakable promise," Zuke said.

"I didn't give my word!" Star protested.

"I made the promise for all of us. It's your promise, too," Zuke said firmly.

Star kicked a rock into the water.

"That was Old Sage," Cucumber said, peering ahead.

"Where?" Toffee asked, catching up.

"He went around that corner," Star said, pointing.

"What business could he have at the Black Castle?" Zuke wondered aloud.


They boarded Zuke's boat. The prince hesitated, eyeing the mess on deck with distaste.

"Are you defying the king's order?" Zuke asked.

The prince rolled his eyes and reluctantly climbed aboard.

Star, uneasy, looked toward the horizon. "I've got to go home. It'll be dark soon."

"Old Sage isn't here anyway," Cucumber said.

"We have no time to lose," Zuke said, firing up the steam engine.

Star reluctantly boarded the *River Trader.* As the boat chugged downstream, she pulled out a harmonica and played a nervous tune.

"You seem like someone we can count on," Zuke said as she finished.

"I'm not. I'm afraid of everything," Star admitted.

"Sometimes, being afraid is good," Zuke replied.

"Sometimes, my fear keeps me from standing up for what I believe," Star said quietly.

## 11.  Voices from Below and Above

Suddenly, they heard a voice  that came from over the side of the boat. When they looked over, they saw a beautiful golden fish, about the size of a football.

"Pssst! Pssst!" the fish whispered.

"Is that fish trying to get our attention?" Star asked Zuke.

"They have no ears?" the Fish said in a squeaky, gurgling voice.

"Who has no ears? Fish?" Zuke asked.

"Double Yews," the fish said.

"No ears?" Star asked, confused by hearing a fish speak and by what the fish said.

"No ears – for their own noise or the noise of others," the fish said. "Like fish out of . . . forget that."

As the fish slipped underwater, he bobbed back up to make one last comment.

"Wait until they're quiet," the fish said.

"What did that mean?" Toffee asked.

The fish disappeared beneath the surface.

"Do you usually hear talking fish?" Star asked, her voice laced with disbelief.

"No… usually, it's the turtles," Zuke replied nonchalantly.

Star's nerves were beginning to fray.

"You won't be able to stop the war, and I can't be part of it. I'm just going to remain neutral and observe—like Switzerland," she said.

"Like whom?" Cucumber asked, puzzled.

"Never mind. Switzerland isn't neutral anyway," Star muttered, brushing off the comment.

"Why stop the war? War is good in many ways," Prince Concord interjected.

"Pa-lease," Star said, turning to him in shock.

"It keeps population growth down and boosts everyone's economy. Even the losers do better afterward," the prince said matter-of-factly.

"There are other ways to achieve those things," Star said firmly.

"I suppose," the prince conceded with a shrug.

Star dropped her chin, shaking her head at his ignorance. She began pacing, troubled by her parents worrying about her and unsure how she would get home.

They chugged along in the boat with Zuke steering. Suddenly, a bright blue, yellow, and red hummingbird appeared, clutching a small piece of parchment in its beak. The vibrant bird fluttered in front of Zuke's face until he took the message.

Star watched, astonished. "What is that?" she asked.

"Same-day mail delivery," Zuke said matter-of-factly.

Star blinked as the hummingbird darted away. "Is it about our mission?" she asked, still processing what she'd just seen.

"It's for the prince. It's in code," Zuke replied.

Tying the steering in place with a rope, Zuke walked over and handed the message to the prince. The prince unfolded it, scanned the parchment, and began decoding aloud.

"The king says to hurry. The Eastsiders and Westsiders are massing their forces. This news sounds bad," he read.

An hour later, they were still making their way downriver, as they watched intently for what lay ahead.

Suddenly, a reddish-brown chicken flew from the nearby shore and landed on the boat. The chicken, about the size of a bantam Rhode

Island Red, perched on the steering wheel and stared Zuke directly in the face.

Then, the chicken spoke.

"In the land of the fearfully insecure, they do whatever the next person tells them," it said.

"The DoubleYews?" Zuke asked.

"They are leaderless," the chicken replied.

"Like chickens with their heads… forget that," Zuke said, catching himself.

The chicken flapped its wings, took off, and yelled one last suggestion as it soared back to shore.

"Appoint a shaman!"

"What's a shaman?" Zuke asked.

"It's a medicine man," Star explained. "A spiritual leader."

"Can we appoint one?" Zuke asked.

"Maybe you can when we reach the village," Star said.

Further downriver, the boat entered a stretch of whitewater. The turbulent waves tossed them violently, causing the boat to lurch and sway.

Terrified, Star clung to the mast with all her might.

# 12. Warnings on the Wind

Soon, one of the Imps tumbled overboard near the front of the boat. The other Imp ran to Zuke, who quickly leaned over the side and scooped up the wet Imp as it floated near the rear. Back onboard, the soaked Imp shook off the water like a dog, spraying everyone nearby, while the dry Imp fussed over it, checking it from head to toe.

"If you're going to destroy the castle, how will you get the farmers out of the courtyard market first?" Star asked, folding her arms.

"Do we need to?" Toffee asked casually.

"Yes!" Star replied indignantly.

Zuke rubbed his chin, thinking. "They'll never leave if we just ask them, and they won't believe the castle could be knocked down—with anything."

"You could use my blockhead sister as a battering ram," Prince Concord joked with a smirk.

"We can scare them out," Cucumber suggested.

"What do they fear?" Star asked, raising an eyebrow.

"The dragon!" Cucumber said after a pause as if the answer were obvious.

"All you've got to do is figure out how to get the dragon to cooperate," Zuke said sarcastically.

The boat drifted into a narrow section of the river, with the banks closing in tightly on both sides. On the right bank, a burro appeared and began trotting leisurely alongside the boat. Its coat was a beautiful silver color, with a stripe of black hair running down its back, catching Star's attention.

"Hello, Mr. Silverback," she called out, charmed by the animal.

To her surprise, the burro replied.

"They can't see, you know," the burro said, his voice steady and calm.

"Who can't?" Zuke asked, intrigued.

"The DoubleYews," the burro said.

"Can't see what?" Star pressed, eager for an explanation.

"The energy they waste," the burro replied. "They're as stubborn as an… forget that."

As the boat continued downriver, the burro reached a fence that prevented him from following further. He bellowed one final comment as the boat floated away.

"Give them…," the burro called out.

"What did he say?" Zuke asked, leaning forward.

"In-sur-ance, I think," Cucumber said
hesitantly.

Star anticipated Zuke's question. "Insurance.
It's a document you buy to protect your peace
of mind if you lose something you can't afford
to replace," she explained.

"Can I insure my mind?" Toffee asked, tilting
his head.

"Just things you buy," Star said, shaking her
head.

"Can we offer insurance to the DoubleYews?"
Zuke asked, a thoughtful look crossing his face.

"Maybe when we reach the village," Star
replied.


At the Eastsiders' camp, the queen sat with her
elders, watching soldiers drill with swords and
practice deadly precision with their arrows. The
Eastsiders' light blue and white flag, adorned
with dark blue stars, flew prominently atop the
flagpole.

General Annoi stood beside the queen, observing the activity.

"The king has ordered a group of ne'er-do-wells to try to stop this war. They're heading downstream in the *River Trader* as we speak," the queen said, her tone measured.

The general turned to one of his lieutenants. "Send a squad south by boat to intercept the *River Trader*. Bring them back—dead or alive," he commanded, his voice cold and firm.

"Bring the Prince back alive. That's an order," the queen barked.

# 13. Plans and Doubts

On the boat, Cucumber declared, "I think I've figured out a way to get the dragon to cooperate."

"And how would that be?" Zuke asked, raising an eyebrow.

"We scare him," Cucumber said confidently.

"Yeah, right," Zuke replied, his tone dripping with mockery.

"Oh, now I *know* you've lost your mind! Too bad you couldn't have insured it," Star said, rolling her eyes.

"Same as the Black Castle. Using the magic powder," Cucumber said, pacing back and forth as he thought aloud.

The prince, sitting at a distance, finally spoke up. "I'll have nothing to do with this," he said, haughty. "Besides, you don't even know if the stuff exists or if it can do what you think it can."

"We'd have to go all the way around to the other side of the swamp to chase the dragon toward the castle. Not likely," Zuke said.

"We've been upriver on that eastern branch. With your boat, it could be done if…" Cucumber trailed off, his voice uncertain.

"If what?" Toffee asked with a growl, his patience wearing thin.

"If you carry the magic powder inland about four miles," Cucumber said.

"Ridiculous," the prince scoffed.

"Come up with another plan," Zuke said firmly.

Cucumber sighed and headed to the front of the boat, deep in thought.

"What does this dragon look like?" Star asked Toffee.

"No one I know has seen the dragon," Toffee replied. "Only its smoke, fire, and bellowing noises when it rises from the swamp." He waved his hands dramatically, mimicking billowing smoke and flames.

"Dragons collect young maidens, gold, and other shiny things they can't use but that others might come looking for," Zuke said.

"…to attract their food," Toffee added ominously.

"Well, that's two more reasons why I'm not going anywhere near that swamp," Star said.

"I think magic powder might scare the dragon," Cucumber said, rejoining the conversation.

"It scares me," Star said.

"It could be something unexpected—shocking even—for the dragon," Toffee said, beginning to warm up.

"Come up with a better plan—before this trip ends," Zuke warned.

"Yes," Star said. "Trying to scare a dragon into scaring farmers out of a castle using magic powder is not exactly practical."

"Land ho!" Toffee yelled from his position at the bow, spotting the village ahead.

"Now, what are we facing?" Star asked nervously. "Could the DoubleYews be hostile? Might they use the magic powder against us?"

# 14.  Land of the Unassured

All eyes were on the village as it came into view—a cluster of grass-roofed huts perched on a hill, safely away from the river's edge. Several DoubleYews stood on the dock, their dark green fur and flat ears resembling Old Sage's. Unlike the others, however, their fur bore artistic patterns: musical staffs, paint palettes, and easels.

As the boat pulled up, the DoubleYews scattered, fleeing into the nearby huts and woods. A sign on the dock read:

*Village of DoubleYews, Land of the Fearfully Unassured. **KEEP OUT,** if you don't mind.*

"They look like Old Sage, sort of," Star said, more to herself than anyone else.

"Look, the sign says they're uninsured. They have no insurance," Cucumber said.

"I think *unassured* is different from *uninsured*—if that's even a word," Star replied, shaking her head.

The group, along with the prince, approached the central hut. Villagers peeked from the surrounding woods and cracks in their shutters but didn't come out. When Zuke knocked on the central hut's door, DoubleYews on the porch scurried inside, slamming the door behind them.

"May we speak with your mayor?" Zuke asked through the door.

"Oh, he has no time for you," a whiny voice called back. "Come back another time."

"No. It's important that we see the mayor now," Zuke insisted.

"That's what they all say," the voice whined.

"Remember the fish," Star whispered to Zuke, holding her finger to her lips.

The group stood silently outside.

"It's annoying, always being bothered. If we… Hey, are you still out there?" the voice asked.

Zuke motioned for everyone to remain quiet. After a long pause, the door creaked open, and an official-looking DoubleYew stepped out, flanked by an assistant and a sidekick. The official, wearing a sash, blinked in surprise.

"Oh, you're still here," he said with disappointment. "What do you want?"

"We need as much of your magic powder as you can spare," Zuke said.

"Oh, we can't do that. Who would make such a decision?" the mayor asked, shaking his head.

"It's not ours to give—it's community property," the assistant whined.

"Time for the chicken," Star whispered to Zuke.

"I thought you weren't getting involved," Zuke whispered, smirking.

"I'm trying not to," Star muttered.

"We've been authorized to appoint an official shaman for your village," Zuke announced.

"What's a shaman?" the mayor asked.

"An official shaman has the authority to make decisions," Zuke said. He glanced at the mayor's assistant.

"You'll do. By the power vested in me by the Rooster of Shamans, I officially appoint you as the village shaman," Zuke declared.

"Wow!" the assistant exclaimed, wide-eyed.

"You now have the power to make major decisions. You are no longer a wuss," Zuke added.

"Really?" the assistant asked, his voice tinged with disbelief and pride.

"Now, mayor, about that powder?" Zuke asked.

"Well… can we do that? Should we do that?" the mayor asked, turning to his newly appointed shaman.

"Yes, you can. Yes, you should," the shaman declared pompously, clearly enjoying his newfound authority.

The mayor fidgeted nervously. "But we could be held responsible… accused of consorting with the enemy—uh, your enemy, not ours."

Zuke raised his hands to calm him. "Wait. We have a solution for that."

The mayor and his assistant followed Zuke outside. "Does anyone have something to write on?" Zuke asked, searching his pockets.

The prince produced a rolled-up piece of parchment from his royal cloak.

"Perfect!" Zuke exclaimed. He grabbed a charred stick from a fire pit and scribbled some words onto the parchment. Handing it to the prince, Zuke said, "Our official insurance writer awards you this certificate. It insures you against all risks."

"Except, of course, those few things mentioned in the fine print," the prince added, handing the parchment to the mayor.

The mayor turned it over. "I don't see any fine print," he said, puzzled.

"Precisely! It's covered by, um… cross-reference," the prince said, clearly enjoying his role.

Star and Zuke exchanged surprised looks.

"Well, I guess we can give you some powder," the mayor said cautiously. He led the group toward a hut at the village's edge. Nearby, another hut stood partially destroyed.

"Been experimenting?" Zuke asked.

"We call it discovering," the mayor said defensively.

The mayor pointed to two full barrels and one nearly empty barrel of magic powder inside the hut.

"Here's what we have left. Others took some during the night," he said with a shrug.

"Who took it?" Star asked, suspicious. She glanced at Zuke, then at Cucumber and Toffee.

"We didn't!" Cucumber said defensively.

"We should test this stuff," Zuke suggested.

"Looks like they already did," the prince said, eyeing the half-destroyed hut.

The mayor demonstrated how to ignite a small pile of powder with a hollow grass stalk. He struck two stones together to create a spark, setting off a whooshing flash and a small bang. The Imps yelped and backed away, clearly alarmed.

"Impressive," Zuke said.

"I don't see how that could dent a tree stump, let alone a castle," the prince remarked skeptically.

The mayor prepared a second test, this time placing the powder under an overturned bamboo bucket with a flat rock on top. After lighting the fuse, he ushered everyone back as the powder ignited.

This time when the powder ignited, it made a very loud boom, shot up blazing sparkles and flashes, evaporated the bamboo bucket into dust, and sent the rock flying high into the air.

"Boom! Boom!" the Imps yelled and fled to the boat, with their eyes wide open.

"Wow! Now I get the idea," Zuke said.

"Awesome!" Toffee said, as he stared at the smoke.

"Let's load up before dark sets in," Zuke said, looking at the sky.

Cucumber picked up and pocketed the two striking rocks.

"And you are planning to pay us for our efforts, right?" the mayor asked shyly.

The question surprised Zuke. He had not anticipated having to pay. Zuke looked around first at Star then Cucumber and Toffee, then spied a ring on the prince's finger. Zuke reached over and pulled it off the prince's hand.

"Hey! That will get you in big trouble when you get back," the prince said.

"Here you are, Mayor. This should be more than enough," Zuke said.

The mayor looked at the shaman for confirmation, who nodded. The mayor then nodded his head in agreement.


It was getting dark. They were aboard the boat and ready to go. They waved to the DoubleYews who had emerged from their huts. Cucumber and Toffee were tying down the two and a quarter barrels of magic powder onboard. The Imps sat as far away from the barrels as the boat allowed.

"Go in peace," the shaman yelled after them.

"One piece, we hope," the mayor yelled.

# 15. Dragon Hunt

The boat pulled out quietly.

Cucumber and Toffee lit small candles, placing them inside colored glass jars on the bow (red), stern (green), and side rails (yellow). These running lights signaled to other boats on the river, hopefully preventing collisions in the dark.

As Zuke steered upriver, the fog began to form, the running light candles glowing brightly in the mist.

"Cuke, blow out the running lights," Zuke said, loud but restrained.

Cucumber and Toffee scrambled to douse the candles, leaving only one near Zuke so he could see his controls. Zuke's cautious actions made Star uneasy, but she didn't ask why he'd doused the lights.

Meanwhile, back at the cabin, time moved slowly, almost eerily. Betty stood at the kitchen sink, drying dishes. Ty sat in a chair, absently whittling a stick. Bill entered, glancing around. On the verge of asking about Star's whereabouts, Betty watched as Bill stepped back outside. Both were beginning to worry.

The boat chugged along quietly in the broader stretch of the river. Cucumber, Toffee, Prince Concord, and the Imps had settled in the bow to sleep. Star sat in the stern near Zuke, who steered with an instinctive feel for the river.

"You got anything to eat?" Star asked. "I'm running on empty."

"Check that barrel," Zuke said, gesturing.

Star dug through it, pulling out two apples and a carrot from the bottom. She handed Zuke an apple.

"Want half?" she asked, breaking the carrot in two. "This is all there is."

"The apple's enough," he said.

A faint swishing sound broke the quiet. Zuke blew out the last candle.

"Do you hear something?" Star whispered.

"Shhh. Sounds like a boat," Zuke whispered back.

The others noticed Zuke's actions and ducked down. Zuke disengaged the engine, silencing it as the boat slowed.

"See anything?" Zuke asked Star softly.

She shook her head. The night was too dark to make anything out.

Another boat emerged from the bend, a vague silhouette against the dark riverbank. It passed silently without lights. Star held her breath, wondering if the other boat could see theirs.

"Who else would be out here with no lights?" Star asked.

"Better we don't know," Zuke replied grimly.

After several tense minutes, Zuke restarted the engine, its sputter breaking the silence.

Sometime after midnight, only Star and Zuke were still awake.

"I want nothing to do with that dragon," Zuke said.

"Even the idea scares me," Star admitted.

"It's got to be huge, fire-breathing, and more dangerous than anything known. Probably very angry, too," Zuke said.

"Angry? Angry at what?" Star asked.

"From being alone. Only one dragon has ever been seen in the swamp," Zuke said.

"I've heard they live hundreds of years," Star said quietly.

"No telling how long it's been alone," Zuke replied.

"That's sad," Star said.

"The swamp's scary, too," Zuke added. "It's dark, wet, and who knows what all."

"Let's let those two chase the dragon," Star said, jerking her thumb toward Cucumber and Toffee.

She pulled out her harmonica and played a soft, simple tune.

As dawn approached, the others began to stir. Star woke from a fitful sleep to find Zuke still steering.

"We're almost back," Zuke said. "Cuke, what's the plan?"

"We're going to have to split up," Cucumber said.

"I agree," Zuke said.

"Some of us will take the full barrels, pack the magic powder into charges, and secretly plant them in the castle. Grass stalks will connect the charges as fuses," Cucumber explained.

Toffee glanced around uneasily, then slowly raised his hand to volunteer.

"The others will take the quarter-barrel around the swamp and ignite it to scare the dragon toward the castle," Cucumber continued.

Toffee quickly lowered his hand.

"Both tasks have to be done quickly and coordinated. Who will handle the dragon?" Zuke asked, his tone serious.

Everyone exchanged nervous glances.

"Then we'll draw straws," Cucumber said. "Toffee and I will be one team; you and Star will be the other."

"What about the Imps and the prince?" Star asked, clearly annoyed but resigned.

The Imps ran up excitedly.

"You're putting the Imps ahead of me?" the prince protested.

"The Imps go where they want. The prince, well, whoever wants him can take him," Cucumber said.

"The prince goes with the team handling the dragon," Zuke decided firmly. "We can't risk him loose in the village."

"Hey! I can be trusted," the prince objected.

Everyone gave him a skeptical look.

Reaching into his cloak, the prince pulled out another piece of parchment.

"Look, I can provide insurance!" the prince grinned.

The group laughed.

"You seem almost normal sometimes," Star said.

"Oh, I can be normal—when I feel like it," the prince said, laughing.

"It's time," Cucumber announced, cutting through the levity.

He pulled a straw from Toffee's hat, broke it into a long and short piece, and hid their lengths in his hand.

"Short straw gets the dragon. If I draw it, you'll have to loan me your boat," Cucumber said to Zuke.

Reluctantly, Zuke drew a straw. Comparing lengths, they saw that Zuke held the short one.

"I guess we go dragon-chasing," Zuke said, turning to Star.

# 16.  Into the Unknown

Star worried she might never return to her family, and the task's weight gnawed at her.

"I'll need your shirts to carry the magic powder inland," she said to Cucumber and Toffee.

Cucumber eagerly removed his shirt, while Toffee hesitated but eventually handed over his vest.

"At least my boat will be in good hands," Zuke said, giving Cucumber a meaningful look.

At the Westsider's camp, reveille blared as dawn broke. Troops emerged from their tents, readying themselves for battle.

At the same time, in the courtyard of the Black Castle, Old Sage accepted a cloth bag of money from a young critter who appeared to be the daughter of one of the market farmers. Their expressions suggested this was a farewell. Old Sage kissed her cheek and departed.

The castle village and dock emerged from the mist as dawn broke on the boat. The gray sky cast a heavy stillness over the scene, with no movement visible onshore.

"Any final thoughts?" Zuke asked Cucumber.

"Get north and start inland by the end of the day," Cucumber replied. "You'll have to sleep in the open tonight."

At the cabin, Betty and Bill moved room to room at the cabin, calling for Star. Outside, Ty wandered near the house, scanning the horizon for any sign of her.

"Ignite your dragon-scaring charges at noon tomorrow—noon sharp!" Cucumber reminded Zuke.

Zuke pulled out a gold, ornate pocket watch and checked the time.

"I show 4 A.M. sharp. Do you have the same?" he asked.

"I do now," Cucumber said, resetting his pocket watch to match.

Star stared at Zuke's watch.

"A relic from the last war," Zuke explained.

Cucumber handed Star a set of striking rocks.

"Here. We'll find others," Zuke said.

"Do you know where to set the charges in the castle?" Star asked.

"Umm… not exactly," Cucumber admitted. "But we'll do our best."

The prince warned, "If you're discovered before—or worse, caught afterward—you know what my mother, the queen, will do to you."

"And if the dragon catches us before the charges are lit, we'll be his lunch," Zuke said grimly.

"If the dragon breathes fire on the magic powder, we'll be his soup," Star added.

"What if we don't have enough powder?" Cucumber asked aloud before catching himself. "There are still a few unanswered questions about this plan."

"If the farmers aren't scared out of the castle courtyard, do we light the fuses anyway?" Toffee asked.

"What happens to my boat if I leave it on the river? It might not be there when we return," Zuke said.

"What if the warring parties show up before noon? Will you light the fuses too early?" the prince added.

"Stop! If you think about all the risks, you'll never move," Star yelled.

"Now you're talking," Zuke said, smirking.

The boat eased up to the dock without a sound. They skipped the gangplank to save time. Cucumber and Toffee leaped onto the dock, and Star jumped out to secure the boat. The pair rolled the barrels onto the dock and "borrowed" a nearby wheelbarrow to transport them. Cucumber stuffed a handful of grass stalks from the DoubleYews' village into his pocket.

A handbill tacked to a post near the boat caught Star's attention.

"Warning. War begins tomorrow. All citizens are commanded to stay inside until further notice. Signed: By order of the king."

Another sign read: "Ferry schedule canceled until further notice."

Star shook her head sadly at the second notice.

The Imps stayed on board. When the prince tried to leave, Zuke gently pushed him back into his seat.

"I believe you'll be coming with us," Zuke said firmly.

The prince resisted but relented. Star jumped back aboard as the boat pulled away.

On the dock, Cucumber turned to call after them.

"Oh, and watch out for the rats!"

"Rats? You didn't say anything about rats!" Star yelled back.

Cucumber and Toffee waved as they rolled the barrels up the deserted street. The boat headed upriver toward the swamp, while far in the distance, up the left fork of the river, another boat steamed toward the Y. Neither those on

shore nor those on the *River Trader* saw it
coming.

# 17. Secrets and Sacrifice

Cucumber and Toffee hustled along the harbor road, pushing their wheelbarrow laden with barrels. They stopped at a bakery with a "Closed" sign on its door. Glancing around to ensure no one was watching, they knocked. The door opened, and they quickly unloaded the barrels inside.

Four of Cucumber and Toffee's relatives waited, seemingly accustomed to unexpected deliveries. Whether they were brothers, sisters, uncles, or aunts wasn't clear—or particularly important.

One of Cucumber's relatives handed him a shirt from a hook on the wall, which he quickly put on. Toffee rummaged through a cupboard and found a spare vest.

"What contraband did you bring us this time?" a relative asked.

"It's not contraband, exactly," Cucumber said. "We need your help to stop a war. Guard these barrels with your lives, but don't touch them— or get fire anywhere near them. We'll be back in a minute. There's something else we need to grab."

As Cucumber and Toffee slipped out into the street, they bumped straight into Old Sage, hobbling around the corner in his disguise, complete with a cast on his leg.

"Whoa! Hey, if it isn't Old Sage," Toffee said.

Cucumber grabbed Old Sage by the collar. "We've seen you making trips to the Black Castle and returning with cash. What's going on?"

"I've got no time for this. I'm late," Old Sage said, trying to pull away.

"Not so fast. You're coming with us. You've got some explaining to do," Cucumber said.

"It's none of your business!" Old Sage snapped.

"We're making it our business," Toffee said.

They dragged Old Sage into the bakery. Startled, the relatives quickly subdued him at Cucumber's direction.

"What did you bring us this time?" one asked, amused.

"Not what you'd ever expect," Toffee said.

"All right, Old Sage," Cucumber said. "Spill it. Why the disguise? What were you doing at the Black Castle?"

Old Sage didn't answer.

"You're a spy, aren't you?" Toffee pressed.

"Never! It's just business," Old Sage replied.

Cucumber tapped on Old Sage's cast. It popped open, spilling baseball-sized packages onto the floor. Everyone stared in shock.

"What do we have here?" Cucumber asked, his tone menacing.

"Don't touch them! They can hurt you—badly," Old Sage warned.

"This wouldn't happen to be magic powder, would it?" Cucumber asked. "Who have you been selling it to? The queen? The Eastsiders? The Westsiders?"

"I haven't sold it to anyone," Old Sage said.

"Then what are you doing with it?" Toffee demanded.

Old Sage sighed. "I've been setting charges in the castle to destroy it and stop the war, but I've run out of time—and powder."

"Why, you little devil!" Cucumber exclaimed.

"I planned to destroy the castle," Old Sage admitted, "but I don't have enough magic powder to finish the job."

Toffee raised an eyebrow. "And the farmers in the courtyard? What happens to them when the charges go off?"

Old Sage looked down, avoiding their eyes.

"And your daughter?" Cucumber asked pointedly.

"She won't leave without the others," Old Sage said quietly.

Tears welled up in his eyes. "I just don't have enough powder to save them and stop the war."

Cucumber patted one of the barrels. "Well, you do now."

"Really?" Old Sage said, hope flickering in his voice. "Still… we'll need a lot of help. Are you all in?"

Cucumber turned to the group. "Are we all in, gang?"

Toffee, Cucumber, and their relatives nodded firmly.

Old Sage wiped at his eyes. "Thank you," he said, his voice trembling.

"Well, let's get to work," Cucumber said. "Do you have fabric and grass stalks?"

"This powder isn't going to take down a castle," Toffee muttered, but no one paid him any attention.

Cucumber put an arm around Old Sage's shoulder. "Let's see what we have to work with."

"I'll go grab some fabric," Toffee said, heading out the door.

They worked in silence, knowing the risks. If discovered, the queen or her men would execute them as traitors. And they weren't the only ones facing such peril.

# 18.  An Act of Courage

In the cabin, time crawled in silence and slow motion. Bill returned to the kitchen, where Betty sat waiting with Ty. He gestured for them to follow him outside. Unable to find Star, he sought their help to search for her. Betty and Ty rose and followed him toward the door.

Meanwhile, on Zuke's boat, Cucumber, Toffee, and their relatives worked on assembling charges. At the same time, Star, Zuke, Prince Concord, and the Imps traveled upriver. The narrowing river strengthened the current, and an approaching boat escaped their notice.

The Eastsider vessel, its military flag fluttering, closed the distance rapidly. The Imps were the first to spot it.

"Boat! Boat!" the Imps shouted.

"We're in trouble," Zuke muttered, glancing over his shoulder.

The Eastsider boat pulled alongside, archers at the ready. They armed their bows, their red sashes standing out against gray fur marked with black skulls. Star crouched in fear as Zuke stepped in front of her, hand still on the wheel.

"We have to pull over and surrender," he said grimly.

The prince rose unexpectedly.

"Could you defend us if you had more time?" he asked Zuke.

"Maybe," Zuke replied, thinking fast.

The prince moved in front of Zuke, directly in the archers' line of fire. The sight of the king's son unsettled the archers, and they hesitated, lowering their bows.

"Raise your bows!" shouted the Eastsider leader.

The archers, torn between orders and fear of harming royalty, fumbled, raising and lowering their weapons.

Seizing the moment, Zuke cut the engine, allowing the River Trader to fall behind. As the Eastsider boat overtook them, Zuke swung the bow of his boat into the enemy vessel's rudder. The impact snapped it clean off. The Eastsider boat spun out of control, the current sweeping it downstream as its crew clung to anything they could grab.

"How close was that?" the prince asked, his voice unsteady.

"Too close," Zuke said. "One wrong move, and we'd have gone under."

Star looked at the prince. "I can't believe you did that."

"It was our only chance," Zuke said, but Star shook her head.

"I meant the prince. He shielded you," she said.

Zuke turned to the prince. "Do you realize they could have turned you into a pincushion?"

The prince's confidence faltered as the reality of his actions sank in.

Star studied him closely. "That may have been the first unselfish thing you've ever done."

"I wasn't thinking," the prince admitted, "but it felt good."

"Who are you?" Star asked, narrowing her eyes.

"Who do you think?" he replied with a smile.

"You're like two people in one," she said, puzzled. The prince fell silent, wondering how many people he indeed was.

Star packed the charges as they talked, tearing the shirt and vest Cucumber and Toffee had given her into squares. She filled each with the magic powder, balled it up, and tied it shut with a thin strip of cloth.

"Maybe you'll become someone different," she said. "End up somewhere beyond your royal destiny."

"Maybe I already am," the prince replied.

The boat strained against the current as their boat steamed upriver, skirting the marshy edge of the swamp. The Imps heaved logs up for Zuke, who fed them into the boiler. Star worked steadily, packing the powder into sacks, tying cloth straps to make them wearable. The prince watched in silence.

Zuke scanned the shoreline. "With this current, we need a cove."

"Is the land behind the swamp dry?" Star asked, wary.

"It's got to end somewhere. I've heard this place called the Land of the Disrespecteds."

"Who does that mean?"

"I wish I knew. I don't like land. Too many things that mean you harm live there."

"Like a certain dragon and its swamp," Star muttered.

"Them too," Zuke agreed.

"Scary," she said.

Unexpectedly, Zuke improvised a song:

> *Fear the unknown, or know it to be free*
>
> *Your fear can be undone if you know how*
>
> *Don't let it keep you from discovery*
>
> *Face it, face it, you can face it right now.*

The Imps banged on pots with their tiny foreheads, making a chaotic percussion section.

They found a cove barely wide enough to shelter the boat. Zuke tied it off to a tree and lowered the gangplank. Star helped him strap on a sack-pack, then turned to the prince. He resisted, but she swatted him lightly on the shoulder and giggled.

Never having been struck before, the prince froze in mild astonishment.

She slung a sack over her shoulders and grabbed a handful of grass stalks. A last search through Zuke's barrels yielded nothing edible.

They stepped onto land.

From the shore, Zuke called back to the Imps. "I don't blame you for staying. Keep an eye on the boat."

Star exhaled. "Land of the Disrespecteds, here we come."

They moved inland through low grass and scrub, following the dark-watered swamp on their left. Albagulls circled overhead.

Then, they entered the trees.

The tall pines blocked the sun, plunging them into an uneasy shadow. The air turned damp and thick. Their steps fell silent on the soft carpet of needles.

"I'm scared," Star admitted, inching closer to Zuke.

"Just keep movin'," he said, trying for bravado.

She gave him a look—part doubt, part warning.

They pressed on.

Suddenly, Zuke recoiled. A tattered snakeskin slapped him across the face.

"Yow!"

They looked up.

A massive snake, half-shed, lay coiled on a thick branch. Yellow, red, black, and green bands gleamed in the dim light.

"Geez," Star whispered. "That's a big snake."

With a slow, deliberate motion, the snake sloughed off the rest of its skin. The old husk dropped to the ground.

"Just in time," the snake said. "I'm always hungry after removing my tight outer garment."

Its tail lashed out, wrapping the prince in a crushing coil.

Zuke and Star stumbled back, eyes darting for weapons. There were none.

"You can't eat him," Zuke blurted. "He's too big."

The snake slithered closer, still holding the prince. "Oh, but I can. My jaws unhinge quite nicely."

It stretched its mouth wide, showing just how nicely.

"He'll taste bad!" Star tried.

The snake blinked. "I don't even know what taste is. You eat animals, don't you?"

Star hesitated.

"I don't," she said. "But others do."

"Just the ones we're supposed to," Zuke added.

"Well," the snake said, "he's supposed to be eaten by me."

More coils wound around the prince, lifting him higher.

Despite being squeezed breathless, the prince remarked, "I don't think this is the experience my father had in mind for me."

Zuke glanced away. "I wouldn't eat you if that makes any difference."

"It doesn't," the snake replied. "How do you decide which animals you eat and which you don't?"

Star grasped for an answer. "Just those dumber than us, I guess."

The snake's grin widened. "Well, he stepped where he shouldn't have. That makes him dumber than me, doesn't it?"

Star's hands shot toward the pack on Zuke's back.

"Don't," Zuke hissed. "We can't spare any."

"Do what you must," the prince said bravely, though his voice tightened with lack of air.

Zuke gave him a sad look. "Prince, you're more courageous than I ever thought. It's been nice knowing you."

He turned to go.

Star's mouth fell open. "We are **NOT** leaving the prince to be eaten!"

Zuke stopped but didn't turn.

"We've got to go," he said, quiet and firm. "We don't have time."

The prince's face was turning red. The coils flexed.

Star's heart pounded.

They had to decide.

Now.

The prince's feet still dangled off the ground. The snake opened his big mouth and began moving higher into the tree, dragging the prince higher off the ground.

"Wait!" Star said. "Some animals we keep as pets."

This stopped the snake and raised his curiosity.

"What's a pet?" he asked.

"We keep dogs, cats, even snakes around our homes to pet and play with," Star said.

The snake moved down and then even closer, wanting more information.

"What do the pets eat?" he asked.

"We feed them special food made just for them," Star said.

After a pause, the snake asked, "You pet them, shelter them, play with them and feed them?

Who, between you and the pet, is dumber?"

"I get your point," Zuke said, laughing.

"Listen, we're trying to do something good here and you are keeping us from doing it," Star said, getting indignant.

"I'm not keeping you; I'm eating him," the snake said, unmoved.

"Well, we're not leaving without him. If you don't let us go, many villagers will be killed and it will be your fault," Star said.

The snake let the prince down so that the prince's feet were touching the ground.

"You mean," the snake asked Star, "Like in that war a few years back?"

"Exactly," Star said.

"Another war is about to begin," Zuke said.

The prince waddled to and fro a little with his toes barely touching the ground, still wrapped in the grasp of the snake.

"Hmmm, that was a bad time. What are you going to do?" the snake asked.

"We have a plan," Star said, brightening.

Zuke used an old sales gimmick. He withdrew his offer to make it appear more attractive.

" . . . but we really can't discuss it. If word gets out, well, you know," he said.

The snake put the tip of its tail up and rested his chin on its, without letting the prince loose.

"A hard choice: fill my tummy or stop a war.

Let me think," the snake said.

"Take your time. Don't worry about us," Star said.

"Yeah. We're not going anywhere," Zuke said.

"Being the more intelligent one," the snake finally said. "I have decided to let him go and not eat him this time."

The snake let the prince loose, head down.

The prince landed in a heap on the ground.

"Turns your basic premise upside down, doesn't it?" the snake said.

Star and Zuke helped the prince to his feet and pulled him out of the snake's reach.

"Thank you," Star said politely to the snake.

"Come back this way again," the snake said. "And next time, yum, yum!" he whispered, waving goodbye with the tip of his tail.

"Until then," Zuke said.

"Oh, when you get to the fork in the road, be sure you go right," the snake yelled after them.

As they walked, Star tried whistling then pulled out her harmonica and played a cheerful tune to ward off scary thoughts.

The three trudged along. Their loads felt heavier, and in the heat of the late afternoon Zuke, Star and the prince sweated profusely. Star stared at the prince.

"What?" the prince asked.

"I still can't figure you out," Star said.

"You mean I'm not always as you expect me to be?"

"I mean one minute you're a spoiled brat and the next minute you're willing to sacrifice yourself for the cause. Which is the real you?"

"Maybe they're both real."

"I don't think so," Zuke said.

"It's simple. When the queen's around, she insists on me being the aloof prince. Father wants me to be down to earth. That's why he sent me with you."

"So, which do you want to be?" Star asked.

"Whichever serves my purpose best, I suppose," the prince said.

"Stick with 'down to earth'," Zuke said. "It works better with us."

Still in the woods, they came to the fork in the road. The road had two signs. One pointed to the left and read Swamp This Way. The other pointed to the right and it read Swamp This Way, Too.

"Do we trust a snake and go right?" Zuke asked.

"It would seem more logical to go left, since the swamp should be to the left," Star said.

"I've got no respect for snakes," the prince said. "They can't be trusted. I say left."

"Remember, this is the Land of the Disrespecteds," Star said.

"What does that mean?" Zuke asked.

"Maybe it means we should give the snake some respect for a change, by taking his advice," Star said.

"We won't have time to backtrack," the prince said.

A long pause followed then Zuke made the decision.

"Respect," he said.

"Let's go," Star said.

They headed off on the right branch and deeper into the forest. Their sensations of danger increased with every step they took closer to the dragon.

# 19.  Rats of Redemption

The queen sat on a cushion near a flickering campfire, her guards watching her like silent shadows. The Eastsider troops, weary of marching, had set up camp for the night.

"Your forces are moving too slowly," the queen snapped, glaring at the general with a fury that made even the fire seem dimmer. "We must reach the Black Castle before the Westsiders claim the bridge."

The unflinching general replied, "We could send a smaller squad across the river by boat at dawn. They'd reach the castle first."

"Yes!" the queen said, her voice sharp as a blade. "Take the castle while the main force holds the Westsiders near the bridge. That's a plan worthy of my command."

"The main force should be positioned by noon tomorrow," the general added.

"And the squad dispatched south?" the queen demanded, her eyes narrowing.

"They will meet the others at the castle in time with the powder."

The queen's lips curled into a sly smile. "Perfect. I'll join the squad at the village. Together, we'll secure the Black Castle before the Westsiders even have a chance." With a swirl of her dark cloak, she turned on her heel, her guards falling into step behind her as she marched toward her tent.

Deeper into the dragon's woods, the moonlight barely reached the ground, shadows twisting around the travelers like ghostly vines. Star shivered, the damp air soaking into her clothes, and softly sang a tune to soothe her nerves.

"The dark shouldn't scare you

Now that the light is gone,

It's the same place, you know,

And soon will come the dawn."

Her voice trembled initially, but soon, the prince joined in, his low voice surprising her. Even Zuke hummed along. Their shared song filled the woods with fragile courage, turning the looming trees into quiet spectators.

As they moved, the ground grew wetter, their boots squelching in the marsh. Star stumbled and clung to Zuke's arm. "Shouldn't we stop for the night?" she asked, her voice small.

"We don't know how far we have to go," Zuke replied. "Better keep moving."

The prince grumbled. "We can barely see."

A sudden rustling in the underbrush froze them. The sound of squeaks followed, faint but growing louder.

"What's that?" Star whispered, gripping Zuke's sleeve.

Zuke scanned the darkness, his voice grim. "Remember what Cucumber said about rats?"

The prince muttered, "I was hoping he was exaggerating."

Out of the leaves burst a swarm of rats, their glowing red eyes gleaming like embers. The enormous rat stepped forward, his sharp teeth flashing. "Why are you in our woods?" he hissed, his voice slick and sharp.

Star tried to answer, but Zuke raised a hand, his voice steady. "We're here to see the dragon."

The rats exchanged uneasy glances. "The dragon is dangerous," the lead rat sneered. "What could you possibly want with him?"

"We need his help," Star said, her voice shaking.

The lead rat laughed, a harsh, chittering sound. "Help? He wants nothing but to be left alone."

The rats pressed closer, surrounding them. Star fought to keep her voice calm. "Why stop us? What do you gain?"

"These woods are ours," the rat snapped. "We came here to escape those who disrespected us."

Zuke frowned. "Who?"

The rat's red eyes flashed as he dug through the leaves and pulled out a small, thin object. "Here, try this," he sneered, handing it to Zuke.

Zuke held it up in the faint light. "A… cockroach?"

Star gasped. "That's a cigarette!" She lunged forward and knocked it from Zuke's hand. "Don't touch it!"

The rat scowled. "Scientists made us smoke these— experimenting on us to see how fast we'd die. Now we can't stop."

"That's horrible," Star said, her anger replacing her fear.

"And they kept us addicted, only giving us cigarettes when they wanted something," the rat growled. "No wonder we hate intruders."

Star's heart ached for the rats, their pain evident despite their anger. "We can't fix what was done to you, but we can stop something else—war."

The lead rat paused, his tail flicking. "You're stopping a war?"

The prince stepped forward, surprising them all. "Yes. It's why we're here."

The rats huddled together, squeaking loudly in debate. After a long moment, the leader turned back. "We believe you. Stay here tonight. The swamp is dangerous in the dark."

At dawn, the rats squeaked a loud alarm, waking the group. "Time for you to go," the lead rat said.

Star stretched, her stomach growling. "Do you have anything to eat?"

The rats brought a leaf piled high with blackberries. Star and the others devoured them gratefully.

"When you come to a clearing, take the left path," the rat said.

Star nodded. "Thank you."

"Good luck with the dragon," the rat said, his red eyes softening.

As they ventured deeper into the woods, Star glanced back. "Maybe the Land of the Disrespected isn't so bad after all."

# 20. Facing the Dragon

At the village bakery shop, Cucumber, Toffee, Old Sage, and their helpers worked diligently, wrapping small piles of magic powder in cloth and tying them tightly with a stalk protruding from the top. Each charge was then packed into burlap sacks, about the size of small pillowcases, which were lightly sewn shut to prevent the charges from falling out.

"Pack them tight and fill each sack to the top," Old Sage directed, inspecting the work.

Cucumber, watching the flurry of activity, voiced his concern. "Moving all these sacks into place at one time… how will we coordinate?"

"I've got the plan all worked out," Old Sage said, pulling out a piece of parchment covered in diagrams.

At the Westsider camp, the leader and his generals sat at a field table, their troops preparing for battle. A courier arrived carrying an urgent dispatch, which the leader read aloud.

"An Eastsider squad is moving toward the river," he announced.

"They may cross the river to move troops behind us," one general said.

"No," the leader replied, his voice heavy with certainty. "They're moving on the Black Castle. From there, they could attack us from two directions."

"Send a squad to intercept them," he commanded, and the eldest general nodded. "We'll start immediately."

At the cove where Zuke had left his boat, the Imps were up to their usual mischief. They scurried around the deck, fiddling with things they didn't understand. In their antics, one of them accidentally pulled loose the line that secured the boat to an overhanging branch. The boat began to drift slowly toward the river's faster current. At first, the Imps didn't notice, but when they did, chaos ensued. They bumped into each other, squealing and trying vainly to reattach the line with their tiny foreheads.

"Imps bad! Imps bad!" they chanted in panic as the boat bobbed in the cove, inching closer to the swift current.

As Zuke, Star, and Prince Concord emerged from the woods into a clearing, they heard a sudden blast of fire and the roar of a ferocious creature. Smoke billowed in the distance, and trees snapped like twigs. The ground ahead grew marshy as they reached the north edge of the swamp.

"That noise is coming our way," Star said, her voice tight with fear.

"Stay calm," Zuke urged, though his hands trembled. "Hurry, unpack the charges!"

They scrambled to unload the sack-packs. Zuke, Star, and even the prince worked together, stuffing the charges under a large rock on the swamp's edge. The roars grew louder with every second, and Zuke's shaky hands began dropping some of the charges.

"Hold steady," Star said, placing a calming hand on his arm as she removed the grass stalk fuses from her pack.

Finally, the last charge was set. Zuke reached for the striking stones to ignite the fuses but froze when he realized they were missing. He frantically searched his pockets, but they were empty.

"Here!" Star said, pulling out the stones the DoubleYews had given her.

Zuke struck the stones together, but the first sparks missed. The roars and thrashing sounds were almost upon them. With sweat dripping from his brow, Zuke struck again, and finally, a spark caught a fuse.

"Run!" Zuke shouted as the fuse burned. The three sprinted nearly a hundred feet and dove behind a large rock.

The dragon appeared—a massive, dark-green beast with fiery eyes and tiny, stubby wings. Smoke curled from its nostrils as it lumbered toward them, its fiery breath scorching the earth. For a moment, it seemed inevitable the dragon would toast them where they hid.

The dragon reached the first rock.

The magic powder ignited.

The magic powder exploded in a fierce blast of powerful forces. The blast threw dirt, stones, water, and plants directly at the dragon, knocking him into the swamp water on his back. The rock itself disintegrated into a flash of sparkles. A large billow of smoke rose above them all. The dragon, face blackened with dirt, covered with wet weeds, shaking his head from the ringing in his ears, sat up and then rose slowly to his feet.

"Geeez. Was that necessary?" the dragon asked.

The small group looked out from behind their rock. All were amazed that the dragon was still there. Even more amazed that he talked. But they were worried because he didn't flee toward the castle. Zuke looked at the dragon and then at his companions. He didn't know what to do.

"That was all the magic powder we had." Star said.

The dragon moved towards them, holding the ends of his stubby wings over his ears. He leaned down over them and got his head up real close to look them in the eye.

"Why on earth did you do that?" the dragon asked.

Zuke was speechless.

"We, we, we were trying to scare you," Star said.

"I think you succeeded. Do you just go around frightening, or should I say deafening, poor creatures like me?" the dragon asked.

"You're not poor; you hoard young maidens and gold," Zuke said.

"When I said poor, I meant poor," the dragon said, straining to hear.

"You have young maidens and gold stored up to attract knights for food, don't you?" Star asked.

"What is said by some isn't always true," the dragon said.

The prince, being a knight, became a bit concerned for his own safety. He took a few steps backwards.

"For food?" he asked.

"You're a knight aren't you?" Star asked, looking at the prince, teasing him a bit.

The prince nervously shook his head meaning no.

Still somewhat deaf, the dragon said to the prince, "I have no knights."

"What do you eat then?" Star asked.

"Marsh grass and bark off young trees," the dragon said.

"Is that why you're so ornery?" Zuke asked.

"Never thought of it that way," the dragon said, somewhat puzzled. "Perhaps."

"How did you make that big noise?" the dragon asked, sitting down in front of them.

"Magic powder," Star said.

"Bad magic, I'd call it. Dangerous stuff. But we stray from the subject," the dragon said.

"What is the subject?" Star asked, as the dragon loomed over her.

"Why did you want to scare me?" the dragon asked.

"So you would run toward the castle and scare out the farmers," Zuke said.

"You wanted to scare me so I would scare the farmers? You three are really nasty," the dragon said, not fully understanding. The dragon pointed a stubby wing toward the prince and asked, "Is he a knight?"

"No, he's a prince," Zuke said quickly.

The dragon got up, walked over and looked closely at the prince.

"Aren't princes usually knights?" the dragon asked.

The dragon walked over and looked closely at Star.

"Are you a young maiden?" he asked.

"Yes," Star said.

"You want to stay with me in the swamp?" the dragon asked.

"No, thanks. We need to blow up the castle," Star said.

The dragon gave her a doubtful look.

"So you scare me, to scare farmers, so you can blow up the castle," the dragon said. "You are not very nice!"

As he thought about what they had done to him, the dragon got upset and became menacing.

"Wait," Zuke said. "We're not getting our point across here – at all."

"Help me out here," Zuke said, looking to Star.

"We're trying to prevent a war," Star said.

"Not the Eastsiders and Westsiders again?" the dragon asked, after a long pause.

"Exactly," Zuke said.

The dragon stood up and started pacing to and fro. Zuke, Star, and the prince started to fidget nervously.

"They've been warring for over a hundred years, and nothing ever changes. Why bother to stop them now?" the dragon asked.

Zuke looked the dragon up and down, measuring his size and possibly his age.

"Because the game has changed!" Star said. "They have magic powder."

The dragon cocked his head, as he began to understand.

"Both sides want the Black Castle so they can rule the countryside," Zuke said.

"Can they rule with this magic powder?" the dragon asked.

"Yes," Zuke said. "By hurling magic powder all over the countryside, from the castle's turrets and probably into your swamp."

"That's not good," the dragon said. "Why didn't you just come to me and ask for help?"

After a pause, Star tried to answer.

"We're guilty of believing what others said about you, without checking for ourselves," she said.

"You're right," Zuke said. "We based our entire plan on what someone told us."

"A sobering thought," the prince said.

"Well, I won't help you now," the dragon said.

"Even if our intentions are good?" Star said.

"With no castle in this area, my worth as a dragon will be completely gone. I want nothing to do with the war. So I will just stay on this side of the swamp.”

“We’re finished. We’ve failed,” Zuke said.

The prince got caught up in the moment.

“What if I could get you a young maiden who will stay with you, at least for a while, and some gold?” the prince asked. “Would you help us save the castle then?”

The dragon was excited about the prospect of having his own possessions.

“That would make me one fine dragon, even without a castle nearby.”

“Can you do that?” Star asked, turning to the prince.

“I’m the next king, aren’t I?” the prince said.

The dragon thought about the possibilities.

“If you promise to keep your end of the bargain, I’ll do as you ask,” the dragon said.

"I promise," the prince said.

"Why complicate his life with possessions?" Star whispered, moving close to Zuke. "His life is so simple."

"Living simple is good, but simply living alone is not," Zuke said.

"What next?" the prince asked, moving up beside them.

"Not much. We're going to miss the action," Zuke said.

"Why miss the action?" the dragon asked.

"By the time we return to my boat and get back to the village, the war could be over," Zuke said.

"I can lead you directly there, through the swamp," the dragon said.

Zuke juggled thoughts about how he would get back to get his boat, the Imps being with the boat, going into the swamp with the dragon, and more.

"What do you think?" Zuke asked.

"Let's do it!" Star yelled.

"I'm in," the prince said.

"All right then. We'll try it," Zuke said.

The dragon turned and led the way into the swamp. Zuke, Star, and the Prince followed, watching where they stepped. The swamp was a dark and dank place.

# 21. Rivers, Rats, Rising Danger

The Eastsider squad arrived at the riverbank on their side of the territory. Their boat docked beside a low rock wall, allowing them to step easily onto the shore. Each member carried a weapon—clubs, spears, or bows with arrows. On the opposite shore, the queen and her entourage waited. When the twelve Eastsiders joined them, they all began marching toward the Black Castle.

"Any word from the squad retrieving the magic powder?" the queen asked.

"They haven't returned yet. They were ordered to meet us at the castle," the squad leader replied.

In the swamp, Zuke, Star, the prince, and the dragon slogged through muddy waters, swatting away buzzing insects and dodging hanging moss. Shadows shifted ominously, hinting at unseen creatures lurking just out of view.

Meanwhile, a dozen Westsiders rowed a small, overcrowded boat toward the center of the river. Their light-blue fur and pale yellow cornflower patterns identified them as soldiers. Ten rowed, one served as lookout, and one steered with the rudder. About halfway across the river, Zuke's unattended boat appeared around a bend, veering wildly in the strong current. The Imps on board scrambled to control it.

"Bad ones! Bad ones!" the Imps shouted, peeking over the gunwale at the Westsiders.

The Imp at the tiller overcompensated, sending the boat zigzagging.

"Left! Right!" the Imps screeched, bumping the tiller erratically. Zuke's boat wove closer to the Westsiders, who now panicked. Seeing no escape, they jumped into the water moments before Zuke's boat splintered theirs in half. The Westsiders swam frantically back to shore while the Imps celebrated their unintended victory.

Although this delay hindered one squad, the main Westsider force was already advancing steadily toward the bridge.

The Eastsiders' main force, heavily laden with carts and supplies, marched steadily but slowly toward the same bridge.

Back in the swamp, Star, Zuke, the prince, and the dragon trudged through ankle-deep water, quickly becoming calf-deep. The trees blocked much sunlight, making the humid air feel heavier. Star swatted mosquitoes and wiped the sweat from her brow. Zuke and the prince looked equally miserable in their thick fur.

"Does this get any deeper?" Zuke called to the dragon. The dragon didn't respond, his hearing still impaired.

Unaware of the danger ahead, they approached a swirling pool of water. Without warning, Zuke was sucked under by a whirlpool. Star, the only one to notice, hesitated for a second. Grabbing a tree branch for support, she bent her knees, submerged herself, and reached for Zuke. Her fingers gripped his ear, and she hauled him back to safety.

Gasping on solid ground, Zuke looked at Star, both amazed and grateful.

"That took courage," Zuke said.

Star brushed off his praise. "It wasn't courage. I wasn't scared, and it was easy. Anyone could've done it. Now, come on! We're falling behind!"

The dragon, far ahead, was barely visible through the dense trees.

"Hey! Slow down!" Star shouted, but the dragon didn't seem to hear her.

# 22.  Saved from Quicksand

The dragon continued forging ahead, each stride pulling him farther from the group. His long legs powered through the swamp effortlessly, leaving Zuke, Star, and the prince struggling to keep up. The mud sucked at their feet, slowing their progress with every step.

Suddenly, the prince slipped, landing face-first in the muck. "Ugh," he groaned, pushing himself up. But as he tried to stand, his foot wouldn't budge. Panic crept in as he realized his leg had sunk knee-deep into quicksand.

"Zuke! Star!" he shouted, his voice trembling.

Hearing the distress, Zuke and Star skidded to a halt and turned back. The prince flailed, his movements making the ground beneath him churn and sink faster.

"Stay back!" the prince warned, his voice tinged with fear. "I'm sinking!"

"Quicksand!" Star shouted, her eyes darting around the clearing for anything to help. Zuke hesitated, then scanned the area. The towering trees offered no low branches, and the ground cover was a useless tangle of ferns and vines. Star yanked at her shoelaces, fumbling to tie them together, but the makeshift cord fell laughably short.

The prince's legs disappeared beneath the surface. "Not good!" he exclaimed, his voice quivering as the quicksand crept higher.

"Don't move! You'll sink faster!" Zuke yelled, his face tight with urgency.

"Too late for that advice," the prince muttered, now chest-deep and sinking slowly. He forced a shaky laugh. "The king's gonna be distraught."

Star's heart pounded as the mud reached his armpits. "We have to do something!" she said, her voice cracking with desperation.

But just as the prince's chin touched the surface, a shadow fell over them. The dragon reappeared, his massive frame blocking the faint sunlight. Without hesitation, the dragon stepped into the clearing, his stubby wings extending with surprising dexterity. The prince's wide eyes locked onto the outstretched wing as it reached him.

"Grab hold!" Zuke shouted.

The prince latched onto the dragon's wing with both hands, gasping as the dragon heaved backward. Mud slurped and hissed as the quicksand released its grip, dragging the prince free.

Covered in muck and panting, the prince flopped onto solid ground. "Okay," he said between breaths, "I owe him another favor."

Then, the dragon dragged the prince to solid
ground.

"Sorry... forgot to mention the quicksand," the
dragon said.

The prince leaned against a tree, panting to
recover.


After a brief rest, they pressed on into an even
denser part of the swamp. The trees loomed
closer, their thick canopy blocking almost all
light. The air grew heavy with moisture, and the
murky ground squelched underfoot.

The dragon led the way, carefully breaking a
trail through the dense undergrowth. Without
warning, a deafening roar erupted ahead,
followed by a burst of flame and smoke that
shot out of a hidden clearing. The blast
whooshed over their heads, scorching the air.

Star and the prince dove to the ground in panic.
Zuke ducked, clutching his pack tightly. The

dragon, however, barely flinched and instead rolled his eyes.

"Mom, stop it!" the dragon yelled. "It's me... and some friends."

From deeper within the clearing, a rumbling voice answered, tinged with skepticism.

"Did you finally find a young maiden, dear?" Mom asked.

"Uh, one, but she's not here to stay," the dragon mumbled.

"Gold?" Mom asked expectantly.

"Not yet," the dragon admitted, embarrassed.

Star sat up, still wide-eyed.

"I thought you were alone," she said.

"In many ways, I am," the dragon replied wistfully.

"Why'd you bring them?" Mom snapped. "Now our secret lair isn't a secret anymore."

"We're just passing through," the dragon said quickly.

"We're on our way to stop a war," Zuke added.

"Well, isn't that nice," Mom said dismissively. "Have a nice day, dear."

Star, Zuke, and the prince exchanged wary glances before hurrying to follow the dragon as he lumbered onward.

Meanwhile, back at the cabin, Bill, Betty, and Ty searched frantically for Star. Still moving in slow motion and silence, their furrowed brows showed mounting concern as they expanded their search radius.

At the bakery shop, Old Sage, Cucumber, Toffee, and their relatives had finished packing the last of the magic powder charges. Each sack was carefully sewn shut, ready for transport.

A villager burst into the shop, his face pale with urgency.

"Old Sage!" he called.

"Right here," Old Sage answered, turning from the table.

"I just saw the queen meeting a squad of Eastsiders," the villager said.

"What's new about that?" Old Sage asked, narrowing his eyes.

"On this side of the river," the villager clarified.

Old Sage froze, then slammed his fist on the table.

"Whoa. That's trouble! The castle! Oh, it's getting worse. Hurry, men. We don't have much time!"

Grabbing a small parchment, Old Sage scribbled a note with a quill pen. He folded the paper hastily and handed it to the villager.

"Send this message to Zuke immediately!" Old Sage barked.

"Zuke? In the swamp?" the villager asked, bewildered.

"You heard me. Get going!" Old Sage ordered.

Zuke, Star, the prince, and the dragon trudged deeper into the swamp, the muck pulling at their feet.

"Stop at the swamp's edge so we can go ahead of you," Zuke called to the dragon.

"Whatever you say," the dragon replied with a snort.

Suddenly, a hummingbird zipped toward them, wings a blur.

"I've been looking all over for you!" the hummingbird chirped in an irritated, high-pitched voice. "You're messing up our record for on-time delivery!"

"Well, you've found me," Zuke said. "What's the message?"

"It's from Cucumber," the bird announced.
"The queen has met a squad of Eastsiders at
the river. Soon, they'll move on the castle."

"You mean the bridge, don't you?" Zuke asked.

"We don't make mistakes in messages," the
hummingbird said indignantly.

"Then we've got to hurry," Zuke said to Star,
the prince, and the dragon. "Let's move!"

# 23. Dragon's Timing

Soon, they reached the edge of the swamp. The dragon stopped and crouched as much as a massive dragon could. Zuke, Star, and the prince hid behind him and peered out.

"We're here," Star said softly.

"We'll go ahead from here," Zuke told the dragon. "In a half hour, you come charging out with all the fire, smoke, and roar you've got. Got it?"

"In a what?" the dragon asked, looking confused.

"He doesn't understand time," the prince said, shaking his head.

"Oh!" Zuke exclaimed.

He pulled his pocket watch from his pocket, wiped it dry with the tail of his shirt, listened to its ticking to ensure it worked, and then held it up for the dragon to see.

"This is a watch," Zuke explained. "It tells time. These are called hands, and they move. When this longer hand moves to here, that's your cue to charge into the courtyard."

The dragon gave Zuke a skeptical look that said, *Are you serious?*

"Uh, Zuke," Star said, nudging him gently.

Zuke looked up at the dragon and finally noticed the obvious: the dragon didn't have hands.

"Oh. Right. Sorry." He placed the watch on a nearby log. "You can keep an eye on it here."

The dragon, who was nearsighted, leaned down, bringing one large eye close to the watch.

"That's better," he said. "By the way, is this gold?"

Zuke ignored the question. Instead, he, Star, and the prince began moving out of the swamp.

"The farmers must leave the courtyard before the castle is destroyed," Star reminded the dragon. "We're counting on you to help stop this war. Make sure you chase them all the way out."

"And beyond, if you can," Zuke added.

"After that," Star continued, "return to the swamp as fast as possible."

"We'll wait to set off the charges until you're safely back," Zuke said. "Send up a signal with three puffs of smoke when you're back in the swamp."

"Can you do puffs?" Star asked cautiously.

"Of course," the dragon said, rolling his eyes.

"Stay here until we're in position," Zuke instructed.

The dragon watched them leave, then turned his attention back to the watch on the log.

"Keep an eye on the watch!" the prince called over his shoulder.

The dragon nodded quickly and resumed studying the watch. He cast a concerned glance after the departing trio, aware of the dangers this war posed to the villagers—and even to his own swampy home.

# 24. Gold, Secrets, and Courage

Zuke, Star, and the prince trudged through the castle's market area, their soaked and muddy pants drawing every eye. Farmers stopped mid-task to gawk and whisper among themselves, their suspicions growing. To them, these three could only be escapees from the dragon's lair.

As they moved past a weathered doorway, a hand shot out and grabbed Zuke by the collar, yanking him inside. Startled, Star and the prince spun around to find Zuke gone. They backtracked, their eyes darting around the crowded street, but Zuke had vanished. Every door appeared shut tight. Then, just as Star's worry peaked, a nearby door creaked open.

"Pssst. Over here," Toffee whispered.

Star and the prince turned toward the sound. Before Star could react, she, too, was pulled inside. The prince remained alone in the street, a thoughtful look crossing his face.

"I have something I must do," he said loudly enough to be heard.

Star and Zuke exchanged a quick glance, their unease about the prince evident. Star reluctantly nodded.

"We'll see you again—when we can," Zuke called out.

"Count on it," the prince replied, striding confidently away.

The prince's path took him toward the palace, his posture stiffening as he left the castle behind.

Inside the cramped shop, Zuke and Star found Toffee, Cucumber, Old Sage, and their crew hustling to finish packing charges. The smell of burlap and powder filled the air. Old Sage hefted a bulging sack over his shoulder, his expression grim.

"Are the charges set?" Zuke whispered, scanning the room and seeing nothing but the one sack.

"That's the last batch," Cucumber answered.

"Hurry. You've got less than half an hour," Toffee said. "The queen must be close."

Old Sage slipped out the door with the sack, moving quickly and cautiously.

In the palace, the prince entered his sister's room, finding Princess Cinnamon at her mirror brushing her fur. She glanced at him with mild curiosity. He whispered in her ear for a few moments.

"This is ridiculous," she said after he explained his plan. "You expect me to live in a swamp—with a dragon? Have you lost your mind?"

"It's only temporary," the prince said, maintaining his composure. "The dragon needs gold and a young maiden. That's you."

Princess Cinnamon's eyes narrowed. "Young maiden?"

"You know, to attract knights—noble ones who will fight to rescue you," the prince said, his tone almost too persuasive. "It's your best chance to find the husband of your dreams."

Cinnamon hesitated. "If Father agrees to give you the gold, I'll think about it," she said.

The prince smiled, bowing slightly before hurrying out, though his expression darkened with the weight of convincing the king.

Arriving at the castle, Old Sage hurried down the street, his steps purposeful but wary. He vanished inside the castle just as the queen and her entourage rounded the corner at the opposite end of the street. Her guards marched in tight formation around her, their weapons gleaming in the midday sun. The queen swept into the castle, her commanding presence daring anyone to challenge her.

She ascended the turret stairs, her flowing robe trailing behind.

Meanwhile, the prince entered the king's chambers. The king sat on his throne, reviewing documents handed to him by a distracted counselor.

"My son!" the king said warmly. "Have your companions stopped the war?"

"They're working on it," the prince replied. "But I need something from you to ensure their success."

The king barely looked up. "What is it?"

"Gold. A wheelbarrow full," the prince said plainly.

The king's quill froze mid-signature. He looked up, his brows furrowed. "For what purpose?"

"To give to the dragon," the prince said.

The king's mouth opened, closed, then opened again. "You wish to buy the dragon?"

"No, Father. The dragon needs gold—and a maiden. It's…a dowry," the prince said, fumbling slightly.

The king looked appalled. "A dowry? You're marrying the dragon?"

"Of course not! Cinnamon and the gold will stay with the dragon temporarily. It's part of a plan to stop the war," the prince said, his voice firm despite his father's incredulity.

The king leaned back, observing his son. "Are you certain about this?"

"Yes, Father. Trust me," the prince said, his tone carrying a newfound confidence.

After a long pause, the king sighed. "Take the gold. But do not tell the queen or Cinnamon about it."

"Thank you, Father," the prince said, bowing low.

As the prince turned to leave, the king called after him. "Where is your ring?"

The prince hesitated. "I…lost it," he said, hurrying out before his father could question him further.

The king frowned, then chuckled softly, shaking his head.

Back at the shop, Old Sage returned empty-handed, panting as he shut the door behind him.

"Did the Eastsiders see you?" Cucumber asked.

"No," Old Sage said between breaths.

"What if the queen's men find the charges?" Toffee asked.

"They'll only have time to remove a few, even if they do," Old Sage replied grimly.

Star's face betrayed her fear. "I'm not going with you," she said, her voice trembling.

Old Sage placed a hand on her shoulder. "When the time comes, remember what we discussed. You'll find the courage you need."

Star nodded but looked uncertain. "I just want to go home."

"I'm afraid the ferries won't run until this is over," Old Sage said.

Star sighed deeply, her worry growing as the seconds ticked away.

# 25.  Claimed but Not Conquered

Old Sage emptied a handful of spare stalks onto the table, their hollow stems clinking faintly.

"Are the fuses all in place?" Cucumber asked, leaning in with a serious expression.

"They're ready," Old Sage said, nodding as he adjusted the crude map etched in magic powder dust on the table.

The door creaked open, and the prince burst into the shop. He winked at Zuke and Star, a confident smirk on his face, and joined the group huddled around the table. Flint stones were lined up neatly nearby, each set ready for action.

"Now, here's where we placed the charges," Old Sage said, gesturing to the map. He carefully redrew the castle layout with his finger in the powder, each swipe leaving faint trails in the dust.

"Light the fuses farthest from the entrance first," he explained, pointing to strategic spots on the map. "Start here, then here, and finally here. These fuses are longer, so they'll give you time to get out."

"Each team takes two of these," Toffee said, handing out the flint stones. His serious tone made even the usually playful Imps remain silent.

"You'll have fifteen minutes to light your fuses and return here. Run fast, and don't look back," Old Sage said, his voice steady but grave.

Zuke grabbed his stones and stood. "To be in place when the dragon attacks, we'd better move now." He turned to the prince. "You're with me."

The prince grinned. "Of course. Besides, I'm the only one with a watch now," he joked, tapping his chest where the king's pocket watch rested securely.

As the group gathered their supplies and left, all except Star, the tension was palpable.

Meanwhile, the Eastsider army marched closer to the bridge. Their ranks, shimmering with the dark gray of their uniforms, came to a halt just short of the river. The general surveyed the scene with a calculating glare.

"We wait here for word from the queen," he announced to his commanders, his voice sharp and commanding. "Once she has claimed the castle, we attack."

The soldiers shuffled into formation, weapons ready, the quiet hum of anticipation rippling

through their ranks. The final confrontation was
drawing near.

As Old Sage and his small band approached the castle, the queen suddenly appeared on the highest turret, flanked by her twelve armed guards. Her crimson cloak billowed in the wind as she stood boldly at the edge, her expression triumphant.

"As the queen monarch of the Eastsiders, I claim this castle and this entire valley!" she declared, her voice echoing through the courtyard.

Her immediate followers erupted into cheers, their shouts ringing out in victory. The farmers in the market grumbled.

"Send word to the general that we are ready," the queen commanded, dispatching a runner who darted down the stairway. Then, scanning the horizon, her sharp gaze swept the surroundings.

"Where is that magic powder squad?" she asked, her tone tinged with irritation. Her question hung in the air, unanswered.

Zuke and the small group halted at the castle's entrance. They looked up to see the queen silhouetted against the sky. Their faces fell, and a wave of defeat rippled through the group. Some stared at the ground, their morale visibly shaken.

"She's already up there," someone muttered.

Zuke stepped forward, his jaw tightening as he surveyed the scene.

"Wait!" he said, his voice cutting through the gloom. "The queen doesn't control this castle yet. We're still free! We've got a job to do. Get to your charges and light the fuses!"

His determination reignited the group. They nodded, clutching their supplies, and prepared to move.

From the bakery shop's doorway, Star watched the small group gathered in front of the castle. Her heart raced as she saw Old Sage break away from the group. He ran toward her, his expression tense.

"What's going on?" Star asked as he reached her.

Old Sage leaned in, whispered hurriedly, and gestured toward the queen standing high above. His hands trembled as he passed her his striking stones.

"You'll know what to do," he said, his voice low but insistent.

Then, without another word, he turned and sprinted down the road, his figure disappearing into the distance.

Star clutched the stones tightly and stared after him, confusion and frustration swirling inside her. Then she squared her shoulders, turned, and strode toward the others outside the castle.

The small group watched Old Sage vanish down the road.

"Well, I'll be," Cucumber said, his voice laced with disappointment. "I guess he is a coward, just like his father."

"I truly thought he'd be different," Toffee added, shaking his head.

Star arrived, her eyes darting between her friends and the castle.

"You've got to take his place," Zuke said firmly, meeting her gaze.

Star hesitated, gripping the striking stones in her hand. "I know," she said quietly, "but I don't know if I can do it."

"You must," Cucumber said, stepping closer. "We're counting on you. Don't let us down."

Star's chest tightened. "You don't understand—"

"We need you, Star," Zuke said, his voice steady but urgent. "You make all the difference."

Star closed her eyes for a moment, her mind racing. Then, with a deep breath, she opened them, a glint of resolve shining through.

"All right," she said, her voice trembling but determined. "I'll go as far as I can."

With that, the group burst into action, running through the castle's entrance and scattering in different directions according to their carefully planned routes.

The prince took the lead, clutching his supplies tightly. They moved quickly, aware of the dangers all around them. The queen's guards could attack any moment, and the magic powder in their hands felt like a ticking time bomb. But there was no turning back.

They knew the stakes, and they pressed on.

# 26. Escape and Castle Chaos

On the other side of the castle, the dragon entered the courtyard with a loud bellow, spewing fire and smoke, knocking carts over, and frightening everyone. The farmers started running, fleeing as fast as they could from the castle. Some farmers threw cabbages and melons over their shoulders, mistakenly believing that the dragon was right behind them and that the food missiles might somehow slow him down. The dragon put on his most ferocious act but at times couldn't help but snicker about how silly everyone was behaving.

On the turret top, the queen looked on, confusion spreading across her face as farmers poured out of the castle, their carts clattering and shouts filling the air.

"What's happening?" she demanded, spinning toward her squad leader.

No one answered. Suddenly, a low, guttural roar echoed, accompanied by flames and smoke from behind the castle. More farmers surged into the open, panic evident in their hurried steps.

"The dragon is out of the swamp and attacking the villagers!" a guard shouted from the turret's edge.

"Oh, that's just great," the queen muttered, rolling her eyes.

Inside the castle, Zuke, Cucumber, the prince, and their crew worked feverishly, striking flint against stone. Sparks danced, igniting fuses one by one. At the critical moment, Star froze at her post, staring at the stones in her hands. Fear gripped her, rendering her motionless.

Behind her, Old Sage appeared. Without a word, he gently took the stones from her trembling hands. Star blinked, her confidence slowly returning. She snatched the stones back and struck them together, the fuse sparking to life.

With Old Sage at her side, they moved to the next post and then the next. As Star lit her final fuse, the others had already completed their tasks and rushed out of the castle's front gate.

From the turret, the queen's guards spotted glowing fuses below and sprang into action. They descended swiftly, weapons ready, prepared to confront the intruders.

Then, an unexpected explosion rocked the castle. A stray spark had traveled down a fuse prematurely. The resulting blast obliterated the lever holding up the iron gate at the rear entrance. With a deafening crash, the gate slammed shut, trapping the dragon inside.

"Small fires are burning everywhere inside the castle!" a guard reported breathlessly to the queen upon returning to the turret.

"They've used the magic powder," the queen said through gritted teeth. "That explains why my squad never returned. They have it all!"

"We must leave at once," urged her squad leader.

"No!" the queen bellowed. "I will not abandon my monarchy!"

She pulled out her pocket watch and glanced at it briefly before gazing at the Eastsider forces near the bridge. Meanwhile, her guards quietly began slipping away, leaving her alone on the turret.

At the rear of the castle, the dragon discovered that the iron gate blocked his path to the swamp. Panic set in as he darted back and forth, searching for another exit. When no

escape presented, he collapsed, letting out a
mournful roar and shedding great dragon tears.

At the front entrance, Zuke, Cucumber, Toffee,
the prince, and the others gathered one by one.
They watched as the queen's guards fled the
castle. Moments later, Star emerged alone.

"Where's Old Sage?" she asked, looking
around. "He was right behind me."

"I think he ran off," Zuke said with a shrug.

"No," Star insisted. "He came back. He's still
inside the castle."

The group turned their attention to the castle's
entrance, eyes scanning for any sign of Old
Sage.

Inside, Old Sage found himself face-to-face
with the trapped dragon. His instinct to flee
was strong, but his sense of duty prevailed. The
dragon had helped their cause; now it was his
turn to return the favor.

Amid the chaos of burning fuses and small
explosions, Old Sage scrambled to piece

together a makeshift lever from the scattered debris. With a monumental effort, he hoisted the iron gate just high enough for the dragon to wiggle under.

The dragon hesitated briefly, nodding his thanks, before darting toward the swamp. Moments later, the lever gave way, and the gate crashed down, missing the dragon's tail by inches.

Old Sage turned and sprinted toward the castle entrance, his heart pounding. Explosions echoed all around as he weaved through the chaos, determined to escape before the final charges detonated.

# 27.  The Castle Falls, War Ends

Old Sage emerged from the castle entrance as another explosion rocked the structure behind him. He joined Zuke, Star, Cucumber, Toffee, and the others as they sprinted away from the crumbling castle. More charges detonated, sending clouds of debris into the air.

"What took you so long?" Zuke yelled to Old Sage.

"What happened back there?" Toffee asked, glancing at him sideways.

Old Sage remained silent, his expression a mix of exhaustion and determination. Before anyone could press further, a sound overhead drew their attention. The albagulls appeared, their wings cutting through the smoke-filled sky, circling above the queen on the turret. The parent albagulls suddenly swooped down.

Each bird seized one of the queen's shoulders in their talons, lifting her from the turret. Her guards scattered in panic as the queen screamed in protest. The albagulls soared eastward, their young trailing behind. As they ascended, the queen's pocket watch slipped from her grasp. It fell, bouncing off an awning, and landed at Zuke's feet.

Zuke picked it up, examining the inscription inside. His eyes widened in shock as he handed it to Old Sage.

"It's my father's watch," Old Sage said, his voice shaky.

Cucumber stared in disbelief. "The Eastsiders must have captured him after all."

Old Sage sank to his knees, clutching the watch tightly. Everyone stood silently, realizing they had misjudged Old Sage's father.

"I knew he didn't run off," Old Sage whispered, tears streaming down his face. He looked toward the horizon, where the albagulls and the queen were now distant specks. A weight lifted from him as he finally understood the truth. "She killed him."

Zuke's voice cut through the moment. "We've got to move farther from the castle. Now!"

Cucumber, Toffee, and the prince helped Old Sage to his feet, and the group retreated to a safer distance.

Farmers cautiously emerged from the harbor area, watching from afar as the final, largest charges ignited. The castle erupted in a spectacular display of fireworks, the magic powder sending sparks high into the air. Moments later, the castle collapsed into a massive cloud of smoke and dust.

Cheers erupted from the group and the gathered farmers. Relief and joy mingled as they realized the castle's destruction had eliminated the primary cause of the impending war. Star hugged Old Sage, Zuke hugged the prince, Cucumber hugged Toffee, and soon everyone embraced and celebrated. Star finally turned and hugged Zuke tightly.

On either side of the bridge, the Eastsiders and Westsiders halted their advance. Both armies watched as the fireworks faded and the castle lay in ruins. The castle's destruction drained their will to fight, leaving them no reason to continue. Slowly, the two armies disbanded, returning to their homes in peace. The war ended before it began.

# 28. Promises Kept

Zuke, Star, Cucumber, Toffee, Old Sage, and the prince gathered in the king's chamber. Old Sage stood directly before the king, his shoulders straight yet trembling slightly. The prince stood beside Princess Cinnamon, who fidgeted with the wheelbarrow full of gold. "You did it. You stopped the war," the king said, his voice warm and relieved. "You kept your promise; for that, you are all free to go— with my deepest gratitude."
Cheers erupted from everyone present. The king stepped forward and laid a hand on Old Sage's shoulder.

"I want you to return to your family," the king said, his voice softer now. "It's time the truth was known. Your father didn't run away. He died in service to the crown."

Old Sage's breath caught. "What? He—he wasn't a coward?" His voice trembled as he asked the question that had haunted him for years.

The king shook his head. "No. He was one of the bravest soldiers I've ever known." He reached out as Old Sage removed the pocket watch. The king held it up for everyone to see. "This watch belonged to the bravest DoubleYew I've ever known," he said, pressing it back into Old Sage's hands.

Cheers erupted again, louder this time. Tears rose in Old Sage's eyes as he turned to face his companions. He walked past each of them, receiving handshakes, pats on the back, and even a tight hug from Star. When he reached the door, he paused, glancing back at the group that had become his unexpected family.

Without a word, he left to set the record straight with his own finally.

The king approached the prince, his expression proud yet curious. The prince, suddenly self-conscious, nudged the princess forward. Her guard lifted the wheelbarrow's handles and began pushing it toward the door.

"Are you sure this will bring me the husband of my dreams?" Cinnamon asked, her skepticism laced with a hint of hope.

"Absolutely," the prince said with a sly smile.

The princess followed the wheelbarrow, tossing a glance over her shoulder. "Well, I hope you're right!"

The prince turned to Star, offering a rare smile. "Goodbye. Be brave," he said.

"Count on it," Star replied, meeting his gaze with newfound confidence.

"Come on," Star said to Zuke, nudging him gently. "I've got to get back to my family."

At the swamp's edge where the castle once stood, the prince and princess waited with her guard and the wheelbarrow of gold.

"Are you sure this dragon isn't scary?" the princess asked, tugging at her sleeves nervously.

"You'll see soon enough," the prince said, glancing toward the swamp.

The dragon emerged from the shadows, his scales gleaming faintly in the dim light.

"Oh!" Cinnamon gasped, her apprehension melting into wonder. "He's actually… adorable!"

The dragon puffed up with pride. "Would you care to see my lair?" he asked.

"It would be my honor," the princess said, placing her hand on the dragon's nearest stubby wing. Together, they ventured into the swamp, the wheelbarrow rattling behind them.

At the dock, Zuke and Star reunited with Cucumber and Toffee. The smugglers embraced Star warmly before heading off down the street, their antics already returning to normal.

"Find a new kind of job!" Star called after them.

Cucumber turned and waved. "Have courage, Star!" he shouted.

Zuke scanned the harbor for boats, frowning. "Not a boat in port. Old Sage must have taken the ferry home to share the good news."

"Oh dear," Star said, her shoulders drooping. "I'll never get back."

"And I'll never see my boat again," Zuke muttered.

A loud boat horn shattered their musings. Zuke's boat appeared, cutting through the fog, with one Imp at the helm and the other feeding logs into the fire.

"Why, you little—" Zuke began angrily, then caught himself. "—heroes!" he shouted.

The Imps maneuvered the boat to the dock with surprising skill, pushing out the gangplank. Zuke and Star stepped aboard, Zuke patting each Imp on the head.

With Zuke back at the helm, the boat crossed the river, and, upon arrival, the Imps expertly guided the gangplank out again for Star to disembark.

At the top of the riverbank, Star turned back. "No one will ever believe me," she said.

"Doesn't matter, does it?" Zuke said with a grin.

"No, it doesn't," Star agreed. She waved as Zuke and the Imps disappeared into the fog, the horn sounding once more.

When she turned, she saw her family running toward her. Ty reached her first, wrapping her in a tight hug.

"Star! Where have you been?" Ty cried.

"I… got a little lost," Star said, shrugging.

Her father ruffled her hair. "You scared us, kiddo. I hope you'll never do that again."

Star slipped her hands into her hip pockets. As her family led her back up the road, she felt the watch that Old Sage had slipped to her during their hug. She pulled it out, studying its gleaming face. A smile crept across her lips as she tucked it back into her pocket.

"You can count on it," she said, her voice filled with a quiet strength.

# The End

For my adventurous readers—
may you always find courage
and keep your word.

www.ingramcontent.com/pod-product-compliance
Lightning Source LLC
Chambersburg PA
CBHW020105310726
48970CB00002B/493